What Grown-Up Fans of MANDIE Say

"I'm twenty years old. I've been reading the MANDIE BOOKS ever since I was seven. My mother started buying them for me and I could consume one book in about a day! I can't wait to pass the books on to my girls when [my husband and I] start to have a family."

—Heather I., Puerto Rico

"I have been reading your books almost as long as I can remember. Now I am twenty-one years old. I have saved all of my books and plan to give them to my daughters when I get married and have children. I really enjoy being able to read nice, clean books, and I feel like I have grown up with Mandie, Joe, Celia, and the others. I look forward to reading MANDIE: HER COLLEGE DAYS!"

—Elizabeth C., Texas

"I'm eighteen and I absolutely love the MANDIE BOOKS. While I am reading them I feel as though I am there with her solving the mysteries."

—Jessica S., Texas

"While I am approaching thirty, I have been reading MANDIE BOOKS since I was a young girl. I appreciate you writing books that are so captivating to young girls (and older girls) and have such a positive message. Psalm 56:3 was one of the first Bible verses I memorized, and I still find myself reciting it at frightening times, just like Mandie."

—Kim D., South Carolina

"I love your Mandie series. I started reading them when I was eleven years old and am still reading them at the age of twenty. I was so intrigued with the books. I was able to see a little of myself in Mandie and her adventures. I can hardly wait for the next book to come out. I am particularly interested in the relationship between Mandie and Joe, being a romantic at heart."

—Stacy W., Ohio

COLOMA PUBLIC LIBRARY
COLOMA, MICHIGAN 49038

Mandie® Mysteries

Mandie and . . .

Mandie: Her College Days

COLOMA PUBLIC LIBRARY
retired
90151000799

#1 in the
Mandie: Her College
Years
Series

MANDIE ®

HER COLLEGE DAYS

New Horizons

LOIS G
LEPP

DATE DUE

AG 1 7 '10		
SE 0 8 '10		
MR 1 2 '11		
AG 0 7 '13		

Demco, Inc. 38-294

BETHANYHOUSE
MINNEAPOLIS, MINNESOTA

New Horizons
Copyright © 2006
Lois Gladys Leppard

Cover design by Lookout Design

MANDIE® and SNOWBALL® are registered trademarks of Lois Gladys Leppard.

All rights reserved. No part of this publication may be reproduced, stored in a retrieval system, or transmitted in any form or by any means—electronic, mechanical, photocopying, recording, or otherwise—without the prior written permission of the publisher and copyright owners.

Published by Bethany House Publishers
11400 Hampshire Avenue South
Bloomington, Minnesota 55438

Bethany House Publishers is a division of
Baker Publishing Group, Grand Rapids, Michigan.

Printed in the United States of America

Library of Congress Cataloging-in-Publication Data

Leppard, Lois Gladys.
   New Horizons / Lois Gladys Leppard.
      p. cm. — (Mandie, her college days; bk. 1)
     Summary: When Mandie and her friend Celia begin classes at the Charleston Ladies College, they must contend with unfriendly classmates and rumors of a haunted house.
   ISBN 0-7642-2932-X (pbk.)
   [1. Universities and colleges—Fiction. 2. Haunted houses—Fiction.
3. Behavior—Fiction. 4. Charleston (S.C.)—History—20th century—Fiction.]
I. Title. II. Series.
   PZ7.L556 New   2006
   [Fic]—dc22
                                           2005033221

A friend in need is a friend indeed.

—Anonymous

With many thanks to the following who were indeed friends in time of need:

First and foremost, my dear friend of twenty-four years, Carol Johnson, who made the MANDIE BOOKS possible, and her assistant, Dana; my son, Donn, for keeping the Web site going, and my daughter-in-law, Shannon, for support; my neighbors Marsha and Rick Frans, who saved me from the ice storm we had during the work on this book; my old-time friend Alma Furman, for advice and friendship; Barbara Franks of CrossWay for setting up all those book signings and for giving support; Lowell Sweat, for keeping the yard in order; Karen Schillinger, my longtime friend who helped in so many ways; my sister, Belle Langford, for her support; my lifetime friend Frances Granger, for listening; and of course—

To all those Mandie Fan Club members who have stayed in touch with Mandie.

God bless you all.

c h a p t e r   1

I must remind myself that I am now a young lady entering college, and my deportment should be in accordance with 1904 social graces, Amanda Elizabeth Shaw silently told herself as she stood in the registration line of the Charleston Ladies' College. She felt her temper rise at the way her grandmother was taking over with the school officials at the desk.

Mandie lowered her dark blond lashes, turned, and surreptitiously looked at the other young ladies waiting in line behind her. They were all definitely listening and observing. She smiled slightly, but everyone avoided eye contact with her—except for a tall, thin girl with lots of black curly hair who stood halfway down the line. The girl met Mandie's gaze, her eyes never fluttering, as she stared. Mandie felt uncomfortable and turned back around to face the front of the line.

Her grandmother was ruining everything as she interrogated the woman behind the desk about the social life at the college. "I want to be assured that my granddaughter has the benefit of social life here such as she has been accustomed to back home. What do you have to offer in that respect?"

"Of course, Mrs. Taft," the woman quickly replied. "We have many . . ."

Mandie felt her face grow hot as she tried to block out the rest of the conversation. She was here to learn—and learn in a hurry—how to manage the enormous family fortune that would come to her someday. She would find her own social connections without help from her grandmother. At least the school was far enough away from her grandmother's home in Asheville, North Carolina, that Mandie's grandmother would not be able to control everything as she had done at the Misses Heathwood's School for Girls, where Mandie had graduated from this past spring.

Her navy travel suit was too warm for the humid Charleston weather, but Mandie's nervousness was also making her perspire. Her right shoe pinched her big toe, so she shifted her weight now and then to relieve it.

If only her mother could have come, but she was not able to travel. She was going to have a baby, and women who were "showing" did not appear in public. Uncle John, Mandie's father's brother who had married Mandie's mother after her father's death, could not be persuaded to leave her mother's side, because they had already lost one baby a few years ago.

Mandie bowed her head and said a silent prayer for her mother. She wanted a little brother or sister and prayed that this baby would live, and that her mother would not go through life-threatening problems this time.

"Miss Shaw." The woman behind the desk had spoken and was looking directly at Mandie. "I believe we have all the paper work completed now. You will report with the other new young ladies tomorrow morning at nine o'clock sharp in the chapel to receive further instructions."

"Yes, ma'am. Thank you, ma'am," Mandie replied with a grateful smile. She straightened up and felt relieved as her grandmother left the desk.

Since the registration was done in alphabetical order, her friend Celia Hamilton and Celia's mother, Jane Hamilton, had already finished and were waiting for Mandie and Mrs. Taft in the sitting room.

"Now that we have the girls registered, we should go on up to their room. Their trunks have surely been delivered by now," Mrs. Taft told Celia's mother.

"I should think so," Mrs. Hamilton replied, rising from the settee by the window.

Celia also stood up, then turned to Mandie and said, "I'll certainly be glad to change out of this travel suit."

"I was thinking the same thing," Mandie agreed as they followed the older ladies toward the door. "I noticed most of the girls in line were wearing something more comfortable."

The ladies went out the back door of the main building and crossed a driveway winding between the dormitory and another large building. Buggies and other vehicles were parked along the way. Mandie glanced at them, saw several young men standing around, and whispered to Celia, "What are those boys doing here? This is an all-girls school!"

Celia covered her mouth with her hand and whispered back, "They're probably brothers of girls who are registering."

As the ladies walked closer to where the boys were standing, Mandie caught the eye of the tallest one, then quickly looked away. The boys continued their conversation loudly enough for Mandie and Celia to overhear.

"Yes, they do say that boardinghouse is haunted," the tall, thin young man was saying.

"Ah, now, I don't believe in ghosts," a shorter fellow replied.

"This is your first year here. Just wait until you get acquainted with some of the locals. They'll tell you all about it," the tall fellow said.

The third one shrugged and said, "No matter, we'll be at the College of Charleston, anyhow."

"Well, *we* won't have to worry about it, but if there is overfill at this college, some of the young ladies will have to stay in the boardinghouse. It could be your sister," the tall fellow pointed out to the shorter one.

The young men discontinued their conversation as Mandie and Celia walked by.

As soon as they were past the two fellows, Mandie covered her mouth and whispered to Celia, "They were just trying to get our attention."

"Yes, I'm sure there is not a haunted boardinghouse here in

Charleston," Celia said quietly. "At least, I have never heard of one."

"We can ask Mary Lou Dunnigan. She lives in this town, so she would know," Mandie said.

"I wonder if she has registered yet," Celia said.

"The out-of-town students register first, so she will probably be around tomorrow," Mandie reminded her. "But it will be nice to see her again after the summer break from the Misses Heathwood's School."

Celia nodded in agreement as she and Mandie followed Mrs. Taft and Mrs. Hamilton across the courtyard.

"I just wonder if there really is anything haunted here in this town," Mandie whispered to Celia. "It's really old, you know, with lots of history about it."

Mrs. Taft, hurrying ahead, stopped to look back and say, "Come on, girls. We have lots to do today."

"Yes, ma'am," both girls chorused, walking faster to catch up.

When they approached the door to the dormitory building, Mandie glanced back and accidentally looked directly at the tall fellow standing in the driveway, who was still watching her. Mandie felt her face turn red and she quickly followed Celia into the building.

Inside the huge double doors of the stone dormitory was a desk with an older woman sitting behind it. A sign on it read *Stop here for admittance.* Mrs. Taft approached the woman.

"Hello, I am Mrs. Taft," she explained. "This is my

granddaughter, Amanda Shaw, and her friend Celia Hamilton, and Mrs. Hamilton, Celia's mother."

The woman behind the desk quickly scanned a list of names in front of her, then looked up and smiled. "Yes, ma'am, Mrs. Taft. Their room is on the second floor, number 200." Then, looking at Mandie and Celia, she said, "Remember, girls, that you must sign in and out every time you enter or leave the dormitory."

"Thank you," Mrs. Taft replied and walked on toward the huge staircase.

"So we are going to be on the second floor," Mandie said to Celia as they and Mrs. Hamilton followed.

"And we have a guard to pass in order to get in and out of the building," Celia commented, glancing back at the woman at the desk. "I think that's a good thing. I'll feel safer with someone checking everyone in and out."

"Safer?" Mandie looked questioningly at Celia as they climbed the marble steps behind the older ladies. "What is there to be afraid of? We don't believe in ghosts, and I don't think young men like the ones we saw in the yard would dare come into a ladies' building."

"You never know," Celia replied in a singsong voice.

"Well, at least we'll be on the second floor, so even if they did come here, they can't walk around outside and look in the window," Mandie said.

The ladies reached the top of the stairway and entered a long hallway with no windows. Mrs. Taft walked ahead and found room 200 at the end of the corridor. She reached for the knob, turned it, and pushed the door open.

The girls eagerly looked past her to see what kind of room they had been assigned.

"What a large room!" Mandie exclaimed as they all stepped inside to look around. "Two huge beds with canopies!"

"Yes, this is the largest they had available," Mrs. Taft said. "Now, I see your trunks over there in the corner. Let's get them unpacked and we'll go back to the hotel for something to eat."

Mandie and Celia eagerly opened their trunks and began pulling out dresses and hanging them in the huge wardrobe in the room. Mrs. Taft and Mrs. Hamilton put the girls' personal things in the two bureaus.

"You have your own bureaus, your own beds, several chairs, and a table," Mrs. Hamilton remarked as she surveyed the furniture. "It seems you certainly have much more space than you did in your room back at the Misses Heathwood's School."

"And we even have two radiators," Mandie said, pointing to each end of the room.

"I hope they don't bang and hiss like the ones in our old school did," Celia said.

"I think you girls should change out of those travel suits before we go to the hotel. I will be changing mine as soon as I get to my room there," Mrs. Taft told them.

"Oh yes!" both girls agreed as they rushed to the wardrobe to find dresses.

"It's much too hot for these traveling suits, anyway," Mandie said as she quickly flipped through her dresses, looking for the one that would leave her feeling the coolest. "I don't know why women have to wear traveling suits, but I suppose the dirt from the train would ruin a nice dress."

"Maybe someday someone will build a train without all that smoke and soot," Celia said with a sigh.

"Remember, girls," Mrs. Taft interrupted their conversation, "you both have a change of clothes at the hotel to wear back to school in the morning, since you will be spending the night there with Mrs. Hamilton and me."

As Mandie quickly slipped out of her travel suit and pulled on a blue flowered summer dress, she said, "Grandmother, we are supposed to be back here in the morning at nine o'clock for our instructions, remember?"

"Yes, I remember, dear. I'll see that you get here on time." Mrs. Taft sat down in one of the huge overstuffed chairs while the girls changed. "We will have our noontime meal at the hotel now, and then we should drive around the town so you girls can see exactly where y'all will be living in relation to shops and parks and such."

"But we have seen the town before, when we were here visiting Tommy Patton and his family," Celia reminded her as she quickly buttoned up her waist.

"I'm sure you did not get overacquainted with the town, and Tommy and his sister will both be away at other schools while you two are here, so it's probably best if we go around town with you once," Mrs. Hamilton said to them.

Mandie was just tucking in the loose strands of hair that had escaped from the hairpins, and then she put on her hat and secured it with a large hatpin. "This lighter dress sure feels a lot better than that heavy traveling suit!" she exclaimed.

"Yes, and we will need to shop for some of those lighter-weight traveling suits that are so popular now," Mrs. Taft said. "Perhaps we could go shopping in New York on your Christmas holidays."

Mandie glanced at her grandmother and said, "But I'd rather spend all my vacation time at Christmas with my mother!"

"We could make a rushed trip up and back. With the baby due in late December or early January, your mother wouldn't be able to go with us," Mrs. Taft told her.

"I'll decide about that later," Mandie replied, hoping to put off this conversation until closer to the holidays. "Right now I'm ready to go to the hotel."

"You girls shouldn't go out in this hot sunshine without your parasols," Mrs. Hamilton said, rising from her chair. "Celia, you have the kind of complexion that will freckle very easily."

"Yes, Mother," Celia replied, getting her parasol from the table where she had put it. Turning to Mandie, she whispered, "A freckle or two might be interesting."

"But you might get dozens!" Mandie warned as she grabbed her own parasol and followed the ladies out the door.

At the desk downstairs, Mrs. Taft signed them out till the next morning. Mandie hurried outside, cautiously looked around, and said to Celia, "At least those fellows are gone. I didn't want to have to walk past them again."

"Neither did I," Celia admitted.

The fellows were gone, but as the ladies walked around to the front of the building they saw several conveyances with young men standing by. Mandie tried not to look at them as they walked past, but she could feel them staring at her and Celia. The young men paused in their conversation and became quiet as the girls followed Mrs. Taft and Mrs. Hamilton down the short driveway to the road in search of a carriage for hire.

Suddenly there was a quick whirl of wind, and the Spanish moss on the trees under which the ladies were walking swooped down and touched Mandie's hat.

"Oh!" Mandie exclaimed as she reached for her hat to keep it from flying off.

"I was just thinking they need to trim back some of that moss, don't they?" a tall blond fellow said in a British accent as he bowed slightly to Mandie and Celia.

Mrs. Taft looked back and said, "Hurry along, Amanda. We have lots to do today."

"Ah, so it's Amanda, is it," the fellow whispered loudly. "And I am George Stuart." He continued smiling as they passed on down the walkway.

Mandie looked straight ahead and muttered grumpily, "I'll be glad when those fellows are gone."

"But if they have relatives here, they'll probably be visiting quite often," Celia reminded her. "It makes me feel nice when they look at me, like I was . . . just something worth looking at. We're grown up now, and the boys are aware of that." She grinned at Mandie.

"Well, I'm not interested in the boys here. I only have one thing to do at this college, and that is to learn everything I can so I can graduate and go back home," Mandie replied.

"Your grandmother probably has something to say about that," Celia said as they continued down the driveway. "Remember, she asked the registrar about social doings?"

"I know." Mandie sighed. "She wants me to become a nice young lady and get married to someone high in society." Leaning closer to her friend, she added sternly, "And I refuse to let her handle my life anymore!"

"Mandie!" Celia exclaimed, shocked at Mandie's seriousness about her grandmother. "How are you going to stop her?"

"I'll figure out ways," Mandie promised.

They came up behind the two older ladies, who were stopped at the end of the driveway. There was a fancy public carriage parked there. The driver was a short, plump fellow in a uniform, with gray curly hair and twinkling black eyes.

Mrs. Taft immediately spoke to him. "Is this your carriage, sir?"

"Yes, madam, it is," the man replied, removing his top hat. "Do you wish to engage it?"

"I would be more interested in buying it." Mrs. Taft got directly to the point. "Are you interested in selling it but continuing to work as the driver? You see, we have two young ladies here in need of transportation while they attend this school, and it would be less complicated if you would just sell me the carriage and continue as the driver. That way they would be assured of transportation any time they wished to leave the college."

Mandie and Celia watched and listened. Mrs. Hamilton frowned and said, "But, Mrs. Taft, the girls wouldn't need a carriage very often."

Mrs. Taft turned to look at her. "I would feel better knowing that Amanda had transportation available at all times. And the girls do need to get out, learn their way around town, and see all the historical locations." Turning back to the driver, she asked, "Have you made a decision about this?"

The man took off his hat, scratched his head, and looked at her. "I don't rightly know what to say, ma'am. What would I do when the college closes for the summer and the girls are not hereabouts?" the man asked.

"Mr.—I'm sorry, what is your name, sir?" Mrs. Taft asked.

"Sam Donovan, ma'am," the man replied.

"Nice to meet you, Mr. Donovan. I am Mrs. Taft, this is Mrs. Hamilton, and this is my granddaughter, Amanda Shaw, and Mrs. Hamilton's daughter, Celia," Mrs. Taft explained. The driver nodded his head at each of the ladies. "Mr. Donovan, you may have the carriage back during the summers. The girls will be home for vacation. It's just during the school year that we need to have it, and when they graduate and are all finished with school here, I will give the carriage back to you."

Mandie, listening to every word, was secretly hoping the man would refuse to sell his carriage. After all, what did they need with a carriage? She looked at the man and shook her head when Mrs. Taft wasn't looking. This puzzled the man, who then glanced at Celia and asked, "Do you young ladies not want my carriage?"

"What?" Mrs. Taft asked and quickly looked at Mandie.

"I don't think we need to buy a carriage, Mr. Donovan," Mandie replied, cringing as she knew her grandmother would come back with some retort.

"You girls are new here, and I say you need a carriage with a driver, so let me handle this, please," Mrs. Taft told her. Turning back to the man, she said, "We need to get to the hotel right now. Could you take us there?"

"At your service, madam," Mr. Donovan replied, moving to stand by the carriage step to help the ladies board.

Mandie and Celia followed, whispering together.

"I'm hoping he won't let Grandmother buy his carriage," Mandie said to Celia. "We don't need a carriage."

"No, we don't," Celia agreed. "But your grandmother will offer him a lot of money."

"I know," Mandie said. "But he may not be the kind who wants lots of money for things of value, like the carriage. I'm sure he worked hard to pay for it."

The girls stepped into the seats behind the older ladies, Mr. Donovan shook the reins, and they were on their way.

In a few minutes Mr. Donovan stopped the carriage in front of the huge, antique Charlestonian Hotel.

"We could have walked here in the time it took for the conversation with Mr. Donovan," Mandie whispered to Celia as they stepped out of the carriage behind the ladies.

"But not your grandmother. I don't believe she's interested in walking anywhere," Celia replied.

Mrs. Taft stood by the vehicle, talking to Mr. Donovan.

"We will be having our noonday meal in the dining room here shortly," Mrs. Taft said. "Would you please return in an hour to pick us up? You can give me your answer about the carriage then."

Mr. Donovan cleared his throat and said, "I believe I can give you the answer right now. I do not wish to sell my carriage. However—"

Mrs. Taft quickly interrupted. "It would be well worth your while. Just think about how much money you would be making: I would buy your carriage, pay you a monthly fee, and give the carriage back to you when the girls finish college."

"I do beg your pardon, madam, but I did not finish my statement," Mr. Donovan told her. Then he quickly said, "I do not wish to sell my carriage, but I will rent it to you for the time your young ladies need it."

"Oh, I see," Mrs. Taft said, and looking at the girls and Mrs. Hamilton, she added, "I suppose we could go down to the factory and buy our own carriage."

"But then we would have to find a dependable driver for it," Mrs. Hamilton reminded her.

Mrs. Taft turned to Mr. Donovan and asked, "Would you consider driving a carriage for us if we bought one?"

"Ah, now, madam, what would I do with my own carriage if I

had to drive one for you?" Mr. Donovan asked. " 'Twould not be possible, I say."

Mandie gave Celia a hopeless look, and as she did another carriage pulled up behind Mr. Donovan's. She watched as some of the girls she had seen at the college stepped down with two elderly ladies. They glanced at Mandie, but when Mandie smiled at them they immediately frowned and turned their gaze toward the front door of the hotel and disappeared inside.

"Not very friendly, are they?" Celia whispered as she moved away from her mother.

"Grandmother would call that ill-mannered," Mandie whispered back. She turned to continue listening to her grandmother's conversation with the carriage driver.

"Would you please come back in about an hour, Mr. Donovan? Right now it seems we must go inside or we'll be late for our meal," Mrs. Taft said, looking around as other people began arriving and entering the hotel.

"Yes, madam, I shall return then," Mr. Donovan replied as he stepped up into his driver's seat. He tipped his tall hat as he drove off.

chapter 2

In the hotel, Mandie and Celia shared a room adjoining Mrs. Taft and Mrs. Hamilton's room. As soon as the ladies closed the door between the rooms, Mandie asked, "Did you notice all those girls in the dining room? They must be from the college."

"Yes, their parents are probably staying over the first night to get them settled, like my mother and your grandmother are doing," Celia replied.

"I hope we don't have to sit near any of those girls who were in line with me today. They seemed very unfriendly. They heard everything Grandmother was saying to the registrar, and when I smiled at them, they wouldn't even smile back," Mandie told her.

"Then I'd say they are not being properly raised, as your grandmother would define it," Celia said.

The girls stood before the full-length mirror and straightened their sashes and bows.

"They are probably wealthy, the kind that think etiquette doesn't apply to them," Mandie said, smoothing her skirt.

Just then Mrs. Taft and Mrs. Hamilton came through the door from their adjoining room.

"I believe everyone is ready now, so let's go down and see what they are serving in the dining room today," Mrs. Taft said, opening the door to the hall.

"I do hope they have something like ham or pork chops, with lots of green vegetables," Mandie said.

"I agree with you," Celia said. "I could eat a big plate of cooked spinach right now."

"We'll soon find out," Mrs. Hamilton told her.

When they arrived at the huge double doorway to the dining room, a waiter immediately came to seat them.

"Please put us somewhere away from the sunlight that is coming in all these windows. It is awfully warm today without having to sit in the sun," Mrs. Taft told the waiter.

"Yes, ma'am, right this way please," he said, leading them all the way across the room to a corner that had no windows. "Is this satisfactory, ma'am?"

"Yes, this is fine," Mrs. Taft said.

Mandie looked around and noticed that most of the diners were looking at them. They all seemed to be from the college, with parents or brothers and sisters with them. As Mandie sat in the chair the waiter had pulled out, she realized she was facing the tall, dark-haired girl who had stared at her in the line that morning. The girl was alone and was again staring at Mandie.

Mandie said under her breath to Celia, "Don't look right this minute, but that dark-haired girl from the line this morning is sitting at the table straight across from us."

Celia subtly turned to see the girl.

"I see, and she is staring at us right now," Celia said. And then she quickly added, "Don't look right this minute, but that George Stuart and his friend and two girls are seated at the table beyond her."

Mandie waited a minute and finally looked where Celia indicated. Both of the young men caught her look and smiled. She felt her face turn red and quickly turned to Celia. "They saw me look," she whispered.

"I wonder if the girls are their sisters," Celia said.

"I don't remember seeing the girls at registration this morning. Do you remember seeing them?" Mandie asked.

"Amanda, let's get our food ordered now." Mrs. Taft once again interrupted their conversation before scanning the menu the waiter had given her.

Mandie and Celia quickly picked up their menus to see what they would like to eat.

"Oh, they do have ham," Mandie said with a relieved smile.

"And lots of vegetables," Celia added.

As soon as everyone had ordered, another waiter came along with a cart and placed a glass of cold sweet tea by each plate.

"This is delicious," Mandie said, sipping the tea. As she set down the glass, she caught the eye of the one who identified himself as George Stuart, and he smiled. She twisted in her chair, trying to avoid the direct view of him and his friend. Turning a little toward Celia, she said, "I do wish I could change my seat."

"You don't need to. There are two huge men being seated at the table behind your grandmother. They will block your view of the young men," Celia whispered.

"Thank goodness," Mandie replied without looking in that direction.

Since Mrs. Taft was in a hurry and everyone was hungry, they soon finished the meal and went into the lobby to wait for Mr. Donovan to return. Mandie saw him pull up in front of the door.

"Mr. Donovan is here now, Grandmother," she told Mrs. Taft.

"Very prompt, isn't he?" Mrs. Taft said with a smile as they all went outside.

They walked out to the road where Mr. Donovan was waiting. Several other people exited the hotel right then. Since Mr. Donovan's carriage was the only one in the parking space, everyone approached him. Mandie listened as he told all the others that Mrs. Taft had already engaged his carriage, so he was waiting for her. Two young girls in the group glared at Mandie and Celia and then covered their mouths with their gloved hands to whisper between them.

Mandie felt her temper rise. Evidently the girls were ridiculing them, but she couldn't figure out why. She didn't even know the girls, but they were probably from the college. She looked at Celia and frowned.

Finally another carriage pulled up and the other group rushed to get it. Mrs. Taft said, "All right, Mr. Donovan, if you would please drive us down to Meeting Street, I'd like to show the girls the shopping district."

Mr. Donovan helped the ladies into the carriage, but Mandie knew she was in no mood to shop. She couldn't stop thinking about the girls from the hotel and why they would have been whispering about her and Celia.

Celia finally brought Mandie out of her thoughts when she said, "I'll be glad when the decision about the carriage is all settled."

As Mr. Donovan drove the group toward Meeting Street, Mandie and Celia listened to Mrs. Taft and Mrs. Hamilton talk excitedly about the shops they would visit. All Mandie and Celia could see were old buildings.

"There seem to be a lot of antique shops," Celia commented.

"Yes, and just what would we want to buy in an antique shop?" Mandie questioned, making sure her grandmother sitting on the seat in front of them could not hear the comment.

"Maybe something for our room or to send back home," Celia replied as the carriage slowed down. "There are lots of art shops. We might find a painting for our room."

Mr. Donovan pulled the carriage to a stop at a corner. Mrs. Taft turned back to the girls and said, "Let's get out now and walk around awhile." She stood up as Mr. Donovan came to assist her and Mrs. Hamilton out of the carriage. Mandie and Celia followed quickly.

"Most of the buildings here in Charleston are very, very old," Mrs. Hamilton explained.

"Even the air here smells old," Mandie said with a little laugh.

"That's the ocean you smell, dear," Mrs. Taft said, overhearing her remark.

"And the ocean is old," Celia added with a slight giggle.

Mrs. Taft crossed the cobblestone street, and the others followed as she stopped at an antique book shop. Very old handwritten books were displayed in the narrow front window.

"Look!" Mandie exclaimed, pressing against the glass to see the books. Turning to Celia she asked, "Can you read that old-fashioned handwriting?"

"Not exactly," Celia replied, squinting to see.

"Let's go inside," Mrs. Taft suggested, leading the way through the front door of the shop.

Inside, the room was crammed from floor to ceiling with all kinds of books. An old woman sat behind a tiny counter in the back of the shop. Mandie drew a deep breath. The place was so small and musty she felt there was no air to breathe. As she paused in front of a stack of leather-bound volumes, she saw the woman rise and walk toward the front of the store.

"Good day, ladies. I am Mrs. Heyward. May I help you?"

Mrs. Taft was leaning slightly backward and squinting to read the titles of the books high up on the shelves. She looked at the woman and said, "Thank you, but we are merely showing the young ladies the town today. They will be living at the Charleston Ladies' College, and I am sure they will have need to visit bookstores." She paused and then added, "I am Mrs. Norman Taft, this is my granddaughter, Amanda Shaw, and this is

Mrs. Jane Hamilton and her daughter, Celia."

Mrs. Heyward nodded her head, smiled, and said, "Welcome to Charleston. I take it you are not from here."

"No, ma'am, I live in Asheville, North Carolina, after several years in Washington, D.C., and my granddaughter lives in Franklin, North Carolina. Mrs. Hamilton and her daughter live near Richmond, Virginia. We are quite scattered about, you see."

Mrs. Heyward frowned thoughtfully and said, "Mrs. Norman Taft, and you lived in Washington. Why, you must be the wife of the late Senator Norman Taft."

"Yes, ma'am, that's right," Mrs. Taft quickly replied, and with a sad voice added, "Norman has been gone now for quite a few years."

"Yes, I remember all the newspapers had stories of his demise and how sad it was—"

Mrs. Taft quickly interrupted. "Please, let's not discuss that." She turned to the bookshelves and began reading the titles stacked there.

Mandie frowned and squinted her blue eyes as she heard the remark about her grandfather.

"Of course, I apologize, Mrs. Taft," Mrs. Heyward said. "Now, is there anything you'd like me to get down from the upper shelves for you to look at?"

"No, thank you, not today," Mrs. Taft replied.

Mandie thought it odd that her grandmother was so short with the bookstore owner. Why did her grandmother not want to discuss the death of her husband? What had happened to him?

Did he not die a normal death? Mandie couldn't remember ever having discussed it with her mother or grandmother.

Celia also heard the shortness Mrs. Taft had for the bookstore owner, and she came to stand beside Mandie, who was pretending to read the titles on the stacked books. Mandie looked at her with a puzzled frown.

"I think we need to be moving on up the street to see the other shops," Mrs. Taft told Mrs. Hamilton.

"Yes, we don't have a lot of time before the sun goes down and we have to return to the hotel for supper," Mrs. Hamilton reminded the others.

Mrs. Taft turned to Mrs. Heyward and said, "Good day, madam. It was a pleasure meeting you." She motioned for Mandie to go ahead out of the shop, and she turned to follow.

"My pleasure, Mrs. Taft," Mrs. Heyward replied.

Outside, Mrs. Taft spotted an art shop a few doors down the street on the other side. "Let's see what those artists have for sale. We might find something suitable to hang in your room." She led the way across the street.

The artist was a beautiful young woman whose name was Victoria. She was busily painting when they entered the shop, and even as she talked to them she kept right on. Mandie and Celia watched her in fascination.

As the painting took on a life of its own, Mandie exclaimed, "You are painting a white cat, just like Snowball, my cat back home!"

The girl paused to look at Mandie, and with a sorrowful face, she said, "You are correct. This is going to be a portrait of a cat I owned several years ago, who died one day while chasing a dog."

"Oh, I am so sorry." Mandie offered the artist her sympathies.

"Will that painting be for sale?" Mrs. Taft asked as the artist continued her work.

"No, madam, this is for myself," the artist replied.

"Do you suppose, then, that you could make another painting of a white cat? It really does look just like my granddaughter's," Mrs. Taft explained.

The artist stopped painting again, looked at her with a half smile, and replied, "I would be happy to. I can have it ready in two weeks."

"Oh, thank you!" Mandie exclaimed.

"Now we must look at what you have for sale today and see if the girls would like any of those for their room at the college," Mrs. Taft told Victoria.

Victoria waved her hand toward the other side of the shop and said, "Anything you find over there is for sale today." Then she continued painting.

Mrs. Taft crossed to the other side of the shop, and the others followed. Victoria had paintings of many different subjects covering the wall and some standing down on the floor.

"Celia, you get to choose because I am getting the cat," Mandie told her.

"Here is a horse," Celia said, indicating one sitting on the floor. Turning to her mother she said, "Doesn't that remind you of our Frisky back home?"

"Yes, it does. It is the same kind of horse," Jane Hamilton agreed. "Would you like that one, dear?"

"Yes, ma'am, please," Celia said, smiling at her mother. "It would look nice hanging over one of those big chairs in our room, don't you think?"

"Yes, I believe so," her mother replied.

Mrs. Hamilton bought the painting for Celia, and they took it with them. Mrs. Taft promised the artist that Mandie would be back in two weeks to pick up the cat painting.

Mr. Donovan saw the ladies coming out of the shop with the painting, and he hurried to take it from Mrs. Taft to carry it to the carriage for them. The ladies looked through a few more shops, and then Mrs. Taft decided it was time to go back to the hotel and get ready for the evening meal.

"Time certainly does fly," Mrs. Taft remarked as they stood on the road by Mr. Donovan's carriage. Turning to the driver, she asked, "Are you quite sure that you will not sell me your carriage, Mr. Donovan?"

"I regret, madam, that I cannot part with it," Mr. Donovan told her.

"Then I suppose we must stay over a day or two longer, Jane, and go down to the carriage factory and buy one," Mrs. Taft said to Mrs. Hamilton.

"If that's what you really wish to do," Mrs. Hamilton replied.

Mrs. Taft turned to the girls and said, "You girls only have to report for assignments tomorrow morning and will be free in the afternoon, so we will go then and see what the carriage factory has to offer. Mrs. Hamilton and I will stay as long as necessary to get this problem solved."

Mandie had been hoping her grandmother would go home the next day so she and Celia could be on their own and do whatever they wished. But she knew her grandmother would never leave until she had the carriage problem solved, so she might as well go along with everything and not protest. "Yes, Grandmother," Mandie replied.

Everyone boarded the carriage and went back to the hotel.

Mandie and Celia quickly looked around the lobby as they walked through the big doors. There seemed to be dozens of girls and their families or friends who must have come from the college.

"More people came in while we were gone," Mandie remarked.

"Look!" Celia pointed. "I do believe that is April Snow talking to someone over there in the corner."

Mandie looked and said, "So she finally got here. But I still haven't seen Polly Cornwallis yet."

"Maybe she didn't come down here after all and went to some other college," Celia wished aloud.

"I hope so," Mandie said, as she and Celia continued to the elevator behind Mrs. Taft and Mrs. Hamilton. "Having April Snow around here will be exciting enough. I'm anxious to see if she will become friends with any of the girls who have been rude to me," Mandie said as they came to the elevator.

"We must get changed in a hurry because there seems to be a dining room full of people already," Mrs. Taft told the girls as they went up in the elevator.

Mandie didn't like elevators. They made her stomach "turn over," she claimed, and she wished she could have gone up the stairs, but their rooms were on the third floor and there was no way she could persuade her grandmother to let her go alone.

Once inside their room, as they changed into fresh dresses for the evening, Mandie talked in a low voice so her grandmother could not hear in the next room. "I don't know what we are going to do with our very own carriage. It's going to turn out to be a nuisance, I think."

"I agree. I suppose we could just park it somewhere and forget about it," Celia suggested. "I'd much prefer walking, if our destination is not too far."

"I was thinking the same thing," Mandie replied. She turned and grinned at her friend and added, "We'll just find out where we can leave it as soon as Grandmother leaves."

They both giggled and Celia said, "I really feel guilty, since your grandmother will have spent so much time and money getting a carriage for us."

"I don't," Mandie replied. "It's time I start taking control of my life. I'm too old for Grandmother to make all the decisions."

Celia quickly turned to look at Mandie and said, "You aren't going to say that to your grandmother, are you?"

"No, of course not! I'll just be silent and let her think she's still the boss," Mandie replied with a big grin.

Mrs. Taft came through the connecting door with Mrs. Hamilton right behind her.

"I see you young ladies are all ready for supper now," Mrs. Taft said with an agreeable smile. "Let's go down and see what they are serving tonight."

As Mandie followed her grandmother and Mrs. Hamilton out the door, she turned to whisper to Celia, "I just hope those fellows are not seated anywhere near us."

"So do I," Celia agreed.

"Maybe they'll become interested in April Snow," Mandie said.

Mandie was hoping she would make other friends at the college and could ignore April Snow. April had always been the troublemaker at the Misses Heathwood's School for Girls.

chapter 3

The next morning Mandie and Celia received their schedule and instructions for the coming semester. Looking around the chapel to see who else was there, Mandie spotted Mary Lou Dunnigan hurrying in the side door. Their eyes met and they nodded with a smile.

"There's Mary Lou," Mandie whispered to Celia.

Celia quickly turned to look. "She's running a little late."

Mandie nodded and turned her attention to the woman at the podium who was giving basic information to the newcomers. "You are required to sign in and out every time you leave or enter the dormitory, no matter the reason. This is for security purposes mainly, but we are also in charge of your comings and goings since your parents have left you all in our care." She straightened her thin shoulders and added, "And we will not tolerate any variance of our rules. Once you violate any of our standards, you will be reprimanded and you will lose points on your grades. You will be expelled should you have a second offense. We are here to teach you and you are here to learn. Please remember that at all times."

Mandie fidgeted in her seat, wishing the woman would hurry up and finish. She wanted to talk to Mary Lou when they left the chapel. It had been a while since she and Celia had seen her, and she wanted to catch up before classes started.

But the minute the woman at the podium dismissed them, Mandie saw Mary Lou quickly walk out the door.

"Oh, shucks!" Mandie said to Celia. "Evidently Mary Lou is in a big hurry. We could never catch up with her in this slow-moving crowd." She followed the other students toward the door.

"Well, at least we know she is here," Celia replied.

When they finally were able to step out into the corridor, Mandie glanced around but saw no sign of Mary Lou.

"Come on, Mandie," Celia told her. "Your grandmother and my mother are waiting for us in the sitting room."

"I know," Mandie replied as she and Celia made their way through the crowd.

Mrs. Taft had arranged for Mr. Donovan to take them down to the carriage factory. He knew the factory owner and introduced Mrs. Taft and Mrs. Hamilton.

"Good day, Mr. McGrady. Mrs. Taft and Mrs. Hamilton have come to buy one of your carriages," he explained to the tall dark man in the office.

"How do you do, ladies," Mr. McGrady said as he rose from his seat at a long table covered with various carriage parts and stacks of papers.

"Fine, thank you, Mr. McGrady. We would like to see what you have to offer in small carriages," Mrs. Taft replied, looking around the huge building.

"Ah, now, you are lucky today, Mrs. Taft," Mr. McGrady replied. "Please come this way. I have just had an order cancelled for a small carriage because the customer preferred we make a larger one." He led the way on into the back of the building.

Mandie and Celia followed the ladies and watched as Mr. McGrady stopped before a carriage every bit as beautiful as Mr. Donovan's, but much smaller.

"Yes, indeed, we may be lucky. That is a beautiful piece of work," Mrs. Taft told the man. "And I do believe we would be interested in discussing it with you." She walked around the carriage. The girls stood watching and whispering.

"Why, I could drive that myself. It's not nearly as large as some wagons we had on my father's farm," Mandie whispered to Celia.

Celia giggled and quietly said, "I'm sure you wouldn't be permitted to do so. It would not be proper for a young lady to do such a thing."

"But my grandmother will have to find a driver for it," Mandie whispered back. She waited and listened as her grandmother continued her conversation with the carriage factory owner.

"Yes, sir, I think this would be appropriate for the girls. But now we will need a driver. Do you happen to know of anyone we could hire?" Mrs. Taft asked the man.

"Yes, indeed, ma'am," Mr. McGrady replied. "In fact, I can put you in touch with Mr. Ryland, who was supposed to have worked for the owner of this carriage. Mr. Ryland has his own horse, which you will also need."

Mrs. Taft turned to Mr. Donovan, who was standing nearby. "Do you happen to know the man he is talking about? Would you recommend him?"

"As a matter of fact, I would certainly recommend Mr. Ryland," Mr. Donovan replied. "He is an older fellow with much experience, and since the customer cancelled the order for this carriage, he is looking for other work to do."

Turning back to Mr. McGrady, Mrs. Taft said, "Then shall we close the deal on this carriage? And if you could arrange to send Mr. Ryland with the carriage to the hotel tomorrow morning, we would be most grateful."

"Of course, madam," Mr. McGrady replied. "If you would please join me in my office, we will draw up the necessary bill of sale. This way, please."

As the girls followed them into the office, Mandie quietly groaned and whispered to Celia, "This means Grandmother will not leave until at least the day after tomorrow."

"You're right," Celia agreed.

As soon as the negotiations were finished, Mrs. Taft had Mr. Donovan drive them back to the hotel for the noon meal.

"We need to freshen up a little before we can go into the dining room," Mrs. Taft told the girls.

"Yes, ma'am," Mandie and Celia said together.

Then Mandie caught a glimpse of Mary Lou sitting on the far side of the reception area. "Grandmother, do you mind if I stop to speak to Mary Lou?" She motioned toward her friend across the room. "I won't be long."

Mrs. Taft replied, "Well, all right, but please make it short. We don't want to have to stand in line for our meal."

"Yes, ma'am," Mandie said.

Mrs. Hamilton told Celia, "You may go with Mandie, but remember what Mrs. Taft said. Don't be very long about it."

"Thank you, Mother," Celia said, rushing to join Mandie as she hurried toward May Lou.

"Mary Lou!" Mandie exclaimed. "I'm so glad to see you."

"I'm glad to see y'all, too! Sit down here," Mary Lou said, motioning to the settee next to her chair. "I was late checking in, so I haven't had time to look for anyone from the Heathwoods' school."

"We saw April Snow," Mandie replied as she and Celia sat down. "Why were you late?"

"Well," Mary Lou replied, "I had applied for a scholarship, but at the last minute I found out I was too late because there was a long list ahead of me when I reported to the registrar last week, so I went home. But that same afternoon the registrar sent a lady from her office out to my house to say I had been considered for another scholarship, so I should come back with her." She paused and grinned. "And I got it! Otherwise my parents could not afford to send me here."

"I'm so glad for you, Mary Lou," Celia told her.

"Yes, so am I," Mandie added. "What are the two scholarships?"

"The first one is in memory of Mr. Robert Haynesworth," Mary Lou replied, "and the second is in memory of a girl named Rosemary Worthington. She was a student here but was killed by a runaway horse, bless her soul."

"Oh, that's horrible. But I'm so glad you got the scholarship. It will be nice to be together this school year." Mandie stopped and stood up. "I'm sorry, but we have to go now. My grandmother and Celia's mother have rooms upstairs, and we have to freshen up before dinner. Can you sit with us in the dining room? We'll be going there to eat shortly."

Mary Lou also rose. "No, thank you. I'm waiting for my parents to take me home. You see, since I live here in Charleston, I'll only be a day student," she replied.

"Then let's get together when you are at school," Mandie said.

"I'll be checking into classes next Monday," Mary Lou said.

"All right, we'll look for you then," Mandie replied as she turned to leave.

"And I'll look for you," Mary Lou said. "Since everyone has to go to chapel every morning, I'll probably see y'all there Monday morning at nine."

"We'll see you then," Celia said as she waved good-bye.

As Mandie and Celia hurried toward the elevator, Mandie stopped suddenly and said, "Let's go up the stairs."

Celia smiled and said, "All right."

As they rushed up the marble staircase and came to the second floor, Mandie spotted April Snow sitting in an alcove with a young man. "Don't look now, but there is our old enemy, and she's with a fellow."

Celia turned her head slightly to look. April Snow was deep in conversation with the young man and did not seem to notice Celia or Mandie as they passed on down the hallway toward the flight of stairs to the third floor.

When the girls opened the door to their room, Mrs. Taft was sitting there waiting for them.

"Let's hurry, Amanda, so we will be able to get a table in a decent section of the dining room," she said as Mrs. Hamilton came through the door from the adjoining room.

"Yes, Celia, please do get a move on," Mrs. Hamilton said.

The girls quickly freshened up and were ready to go downstairs.

"Too bad we can't walk down the staircase," Mandie whispered to Celia as Mrs. Taft led the way toward the elevator.

"Maybe April will go on down to the dining room," Celia replied.

But there was no sign of April Snow in the dining room.

During the noonday meal Mrs. Taft decided she would rest for the afternoon. "This humidity has just got to me. I believe I will relax in our room for the afternoon," Mrs. Taft told Mrs. Hamilton.

"That is a good idea," Mrs. Hamilton agreed. "I am not up to getting outside either during the hot afternoon." She turned to Celia and asked, "Would you like to stay in this afternoon also, dear?"

"Yes, ma'am," Celia replied. "There is nothing going on at the college this afternoon, so we don't have to go out."

"I don't want to take a nap because I won't sleep tonight if I do, but it would be nice to just stay here in the hotel until suppertime, and then after that we could all go for a walk or something," Mandie suggested, looking to her grandmother.

"That's fine. Just don't go wandering off somewhere by yourself," Mrs. Taft told her. "There are shops in the basement of this hotel. You might want to go look around down there."

"Or y'all may run into some of your friends who are probably staying here until classes start next Monday," Mrs. Hamilton told the girls.

"Maybe we'll just sit in the lobby and watch the people come in and out," Mandie said.

The two girls decided to explore the shops in the basement, but they found nothing of interest, so they didn't stay down there long. As they came back up into the lobby, Mandie spotted Polly Cornwallis sitting in the far corner talking to another girl whom they didn't know.

Polly lived next door to Mandie back home and was forever chasing Joe when he came to visit the Shaws. When Mrs. Taft had given Mandie and her friends a trip to Europe as a graduation gift, Polly had been invited to join them. Mandie was surprised at how well-behaved the girl had been, but after all, she was more interested in getting acquainted with boys than in seeing Europe.

As Mandie and Celia stood there looking across the room at

Polly, Mandie said, "Shall we just go sit near her and eavesdrop?" She smiled mischievously.

"Yes," Celia replied, smiling as they walked across the room.

They sat on a small settee next to the chairs where Polly and the other girl sat, but Polly didn't seem to notice them as she chattered away.

"I do hope there are lots of good-looking boys at the College of Charleston here that we can get to meet. It's ridiculous that women are not allowed to attend the College of Charleston," Polly was saying.

"But young men are not allowed to attend this college, either," the dark-haired girl replied. "Though I do think that is a silly rule. Boys and girls are going to get together anyway, don't you agree?"

"Yes, I do indeed," Polly replied, and looking up at that moment she finally noticed Mandie and Celia. "Well, I see y'all got here," she said to them.

"Yes, we've been here since Monday," Mandie replied. "I didn't see you at registration. Were you late coming in?"

"No, of course not," Polly replied. "My mother managed to get me checked in without standing in that long line because she had to return home."

Mandie noticed that Polly had not introduced them to the girl Polly had just been talking with. Mandie leaned over and said, "I'm Mandie Shaw and this is my friend Celia Hamilton. Polly is my next-door neighbor back home."

"My name is Alexandra Willoughby," the girl replied. "My

mother and Polly's mother went to school together, but Polly and I only met here at the college when our mothers ran into each other after all those years. But enough about me. It must be wonderful to have Mrs. Norman Taft for a grandmother. She owns absolutely everything, it seems."

"I'm not sure what all Grandmother owns, but I do know she owns the ship line that we went to Europe on," Mandie replied, noting how the girl could change subjects all in one breath. Therefore, she was probably a nosy kind of person, so Mandie didn't care to get to know her.

Polly stood up, looked around, and said, "Let's go walk around outside. There are probably lots of fellows out there."

Alexandra quickly joined her. "That would beat sitting here in this stuffy hotel," she said.

Polly looked at Mandie and Celia and asked, "Are y'all coming?"

Celia shook her head and Mandie replied, "No, thank you. I'm not interested in whatever boys may be out there."

"I would advise you to get acquainted with boys here in Charleston," Polly said. "Joe Woodard is many miles away now at his college in New Orleans, and I doubt that you will see much of him."

Mandie felt her anger rise. "I am not here to meet a lot of boys, nor am I worried about what Joe is doing at his college. Right now I am here to study and learn what they have to offer so I can earn a diploma and go back home."

Polly didn't reply but gave her a smile as she and Alexandra walked away across the lobby.

"I do believe Polly Cornwallis is the rudest person I have ever met," Mandie said, frowning as she watched Polly and Alexandra go out the front door. "I ought to have learned that by now."

"I would just ignore her if I were you," Celia said. "We'll probably get to know lots of other girls here as soon as we begin classes."

"You know, Celia, I have to admit something to you," Mandie said, frowning as she thought about what she was saying. "I do believe I'm sorry I didn't go to Joe's college. At least we would know him there, and the girls probably wouldn't be as rude as the ones we've met here."

"Oh, Mandie, I don't know about that," Celia said. "I think we'll be able to make lots of friends here, and it is close enough that we can go home when we get an extra day off."

Mandie sighed. "You're right. I suppose I'm just homesick."

At that moment Mandie looked across the lobby and saw George Stuart. He was coming in the front door and she quickly glanced in another direction, hoping he didn't see them.

Celia had also seen him. "There's that fellow who tried to talk to you in the driveway, Mandie," Celia told her.

"I know. I hope he doesn't see us," Mandie said, looking at her friend rather than across the lobby.

"Sorry, you're out of luck. Here he comes," Celia told her as she pretended not to see the young man.

George Stuart walked right up to them and, in his British

accent, said, "Hello, Amanda, what a streak of luck to run into you."

"I'm sorry, but, ah, we haven't been properly introduced," Mandie stuttered, trying not to look at him.

"Oh, but we have been, when that string of moss almost knocked off your hat. I clearly remember that," he said, grinning at both girls. "It would be an honor if you would grant me permission to sit down and talk a bit. May I?"

Mandie looked up at him and said, "I am truly sorry, but my grandmother would really be upset since, as I said, we have not been introduced."

"Have not been introduced? Now, let's see," he said, glancing around the huge lobby. "Maybe I can find someone to introduce us. Would that be acceptable?"

Mandie thought he didn't understand the ways of southern society since evidently he was British. However, she also knew that if her grandmother happened to come along right now, Mandie would be in trouble for talking to strange boys.

"My sister is attending the same college as you are. Perhaps I can arrange for her to introduce us then," the young man said with a big grin. "Would that be acceptable?"

"But she is not here right this minute and we shouldn't even be carrying on a conversation," Mandie told him. "Please understand that."

George bowed slightly and said, "I beg your pardon, then, Miss Amanda. I do not wish to break your society rules. I will have my sister become acquainted with you and then she will be able to introduce us. Would that be acceptable?"

"Yes, that would be acceptable," Mandie finally agreed. She quickly stood up. "But right now my friend and I have to go to our room. Good day, Mr. Stuart." She quickly started across the lobby and Celia immediately followed her.

"Good day, Miss Amanda," the young fellow called after her.

Mandie rushed up the staircase instead of taking the elevator to the third floor. She felt really flustered with a stranger approaching her like that, and she knew her grandmother would give her a long lecture about the necessity of a formal introduction with young men. This place wasn't like back home, where everyone knew everyone and introductions were not necessary.

"Mandie, he's gone, so we don't have to go back to our room yet," Celia told her as she kept up with Mandie.

"Oh good," Mandie replied, coming to the top of the second-floor staircase. She paused to look around. There was no one in sight. "Why don't we sit on one of those settees for a little while?"

"That's fine with me," Celia agreed. "We can watch everyone come and go up and down the stairs."

Mandie led the way to one of the seats and sat down. Celia joined her. She took a long breath, straightened her skirt, and said, "I don't know why that fellow upset me so much. Maybe it's his accent. He is evidently not an American."

"I agree with you that he should not have approached us without being introduced by someone we know," Celia said. "Now that we are older we have to behave that way—older, that is. That's the part of growing up that I don't like. I like meeting new people and talking with them without bothering to be introduced by someone else."

"At least my grandmother was nowhere in sight, or it might have been embarrassing," Mandie said, getting comfortable on the settee. "And just think—we have to live by all these rules until we graduate and go back home. Oh, that the time will pass quickly."

But her world as she had always known it would soon never be the same again.

chapter 4

Mr. Ryland showed up the next morning at nine o'clock with the carriage. Mandie noticed that, after questioning him about his family and experience, her grandmother seemed pleased with him as their driver.

Mr. Ryland was an older man, probably older than her grandmother, Mandie decided, as she listened to the instructions Mrs. Taft was giving the man.

"You need to report to the college at least once a day to find out whether the young ladies want to use the carriage. You will have to check with them on Monday morning to get their schedule then. Mrs. Hamilton and I will be leaving for our homes on Sunday."

Mandie looked at Celia, and they both smiled. They would soon have the freedom of being on their own without Mrs. Taft's supervision.

"Yes, madam," Mr. Ryland said, standing nearly a head taller than Mrs. Taft. He held his hat in his hand and smiled as he spoke. "Whatever you say, madam."

Mrs. Taft turned to Mandie and said, "We need to bring some fresh clothes for you and Celia over to the hotel. Since Celia's mother and I will be staying longer than we expected, you might as well stay in the hotel with us until we leave on Sunday."

Mrs. Hamilton spoke up. "Today is only Wednesday, so you will need enough clothes for four more days."

"Yes, ma'am," Celia agreed.

Mrs. Taft turned to Mrs. Hamilton and said, "I thought we could spend the rest of this week driving around town and getting the girls acquainted with the driver and the sights."

"That is a wonderful idea, Mrs. Taft," Mrs. Hamilton agreed. "I'm glad we do have more time to spend with the girls."

Mrs. Taft spoke to the driver. "Now, Mr. Ryland, please take us over to the college so we can bring a few things back to the hotel."

"At your service, madam," Mr. Ryland replied, slightly bowing.

Mandie thought the man was a little nervous dealing with her grandmother as he offered his hand for Mrs. Taft to board the carriage.

During the following days of sightseeing, Mandie realized the man was greatly impressed by her grandmother. He seemed to be the kind of person who would do everything absolutely right. Mrs. Taft kept giving him instructions, all of which he agreed to. He was to make a report to her each month regarding the use of the carriage, where the girls went, and how often it was used. He was also to see that the carriage was kept shiny and clean at all times. And she would mail him a check at the first of each month for his services.

Mandie and Celia listened silently to all this, exchanged glances, and then whispered about it in their room at the hotel that night. It seemed that although Mrs. Taft would be going home soon, she would still have control over Mandie.

"Now we can't just park the carriage somewhere, like we had talked about doing after your grandmother leaves," Celia remarked to Mandie as they got ready for bed in their hotel room that night.

Mandie frowned as she thoughtfully replied, "No, but we don't have to use the carriage—I mean, we don't *have* to go anywhere. We can just stay right in our room in the dormitory and study."

"We could always get a public carriage when we want to go somewhere," Celia suggested.

"I suppose so, if there is any place we really want to go," Mandie agreed.

"Like to church on Sunday," Celia added.

"We could walk there. It's only two blocks down the street," Mandie reminded her.

But they didn't go to church the following Sunday. The train left right as the services began, and Mandie and Celia were allowed to go to the depot to see Mrs. Taft and Mrs. Hamilton off. The girls were given final instructions, and Mrs. Taft said she would return for a visit soon.

As the train pulled out of the station, Mandie and Celia stood on the platform waving good-bye.

"Exactly *how* soon my grandmother didn't say," Mandie said with a hint of concern in her voice, yet she still gave a loud sigh of relief.

The two girls turned to walk down the steps from the platform to the carriage with Mr. Ryland standing by.

"Since we don't have to be in the dining room until after church services, why don't we just ride around awhile?" Mandie suggested as they approached the carriage.

Celia smiled as she said, "And see what all the ladies who will be coming out of the churches are wearing?"

Mandie paused to look at her and asked, "You really are interested in what other people are wearing?"

"Only to the extent that I don't want to look like a country hick among the city girls," Celia replied.

"But your mother and my grandmother bought most of our clothes in New York," Mandie reminded her. "I doubt that will make us look like 'country hicks.'"

"I know, but New York fashions just might not be popular down here in Charleston. In fact, we may be ahead of the latest fashions," Celia tried to explain.

"Oh, well, if you say so." Mandie shrugged her shoulders and decided to go along with what Celia wanted to do.

Mr. Ryland knew where many of the churches in Charleston were located, and he gladly promised to drive by each one. Services would soon end and the ladies would come out of the churches. Upon Mandie's insistence, he had put the top down so they could talk to him as he drove.

"We have to get down to real work tomorrow when our classes begin," Mandie remarked as they rode along.

"I know, and I'll be glad to finally get on a schedule. It has been so hectic since we came here," Celia replied.

They rode by a church that was finally dismissing its congregation.

"That is early mass," Mr. Ryland explained as he slowed down. Mandie and Celia watched as dozens of older ladies in average dress walked out of the church.

"I'd say most of those ladies are wearing the same fashions that my grandmother and your mother wear," Mandie said to Celia as she watched the ladies walk on down the street.

Mandie and Celia saw the same styles as they watched all the other congregations leaving their churches, too.

"Well," Mandie said as they headed back toward the college, "evidently the ladies in Charleston shop in New York, or they have New York shops here."

Mr. Ryland pulled up by the college, and Mandie and Celia quickly stepped down.

"Anything else today, young ladies?" he asked.

"Oh no, Mr. Ryland. You just go on home for your own noonday meal. We'll be staying here the rest of the day," Mandie replied. "And thank you so much."

"Then I will be here waiting for you tomorrow morning to get your schedule, as your grandmother requested," Mr. Ryland replied.

"Yes, sir," both girls answered as they quickly started walking toward their dormitory.

Finally in their room, Mandie looked at Celia and asked, "Do you suppose we have to wear our hats to the dining room?"

Celia frowned and said, "I don't think so." And then reaching to remove her hat, she added, "At least, I'm not going to wear mine."

"With all the formal do's and don'ts, I can't remember hearing whether we should or not, so here goes mine, too." Mandie took her hat off and hung it on her bedpost.

They hurried over to the dining hall and found a long line already forming. Most of the girls were not wearing their hats, and Mandie and Celia noticed that some who had theirs on quickly removed them.

Mandie looked at Celia and grinned as she said, "For once we made the right decision."

The meal was buffet-style, and Mandie and Celia noticed that the girls holding their hats tried to balance their trays as they walked toward the tables. The dining room employees quickly came to the rescue and carried most of the trays.

As everyone finally sat down with their food, an older woman sitting at a table at the front of the room stood up, tapped on a dish, and said, "Hello, young ladies. I am Miss Todd, and I am in charge of the dining hall. Since this is your first formal meal with the school, there are a few things I need to explain."

Everyone quieted down and looked at her as she continued. "First of all, all of our meals will be very informal in order not to encroach on your study time. You may wear whatever you wish, hats not required, as long as we have no visitors dining with us, which would be very rare. You may eat and leave whenever you wish. We will not have a dismissal rule for that, either. The only rule we really have is, breakfast is at seven-thirty, immediately before chapel every morning; the noon meal is at twelve-thirty; and our supper is at six o'clock. If you have any reason any time for not being able to meet this schedule, you will have an opportunity for a meal earlier or later, but, mind you, the variance in time is allowed only because of any schedules here at the college—not for personal reasons."

Mandie whispered to Celia, "They are more lenient here than the Misses Heathwood's School, aren't they?"

Celia nodded.

The woman continued. "Now we will return thanks for our food." She raised her hand, bowed her head, and said, "We thank thee, O God, for these many blessings at our school and for our food. Amen."

As soon as the meal was over, Mandie and Celia went back to their room, where it was cooler than outside.

"I hate waiting for classes to begin tomorrow," Mandie complained as she plopped into a big chair. "I'd like to get it all over with. Besides, I hate not knowing what our schedule will be until tomorrow. But I'm sure we won't be in every class together since we are not taking all the same subjects."

"That's right," Celia agreed, "since I will be taking a lot of music classes and you will be taking business classes."

"I wonder how many girls here will be taking business classes?" Mandie said to Celia. "Not many, I'd guess."

———————

The next morning, when schedules were given out in chapel, Mandie discovered that only three other girls were taking business classes, and to her surprise, one of them was Mary Lou.

Mary Lou was sitting with Mandie and Celia when the schedules were passed out.

"You are taking business, also?" Mandie asked in surprise, as she glanced over at Mary Lou's paper.

"Oh yes," Mary Lou said. "You see, my father keeps records for quite a few companies, and I'd like to be able to help him. He really has more than he can handle, and if I can learn the basics, he won't have to hire someone else."

Mandie looked at her and grinned. "I'm glad you are. My grandmother says that someday I will inherit lots of business from her, so she wants me to marry someone who would be able to handle everything. But I don't want to have to rely on that plan, so I have decided I will learn it all myself. Who knows? I may never even get married." She laughed.

"Oh, I believe you will marry someday," Mary Lou countered. "But it is an excellent idea to learn the business yourself."

"Well, I know I'd never be able to handle money," Celia said with a sigh.

"And I will never know music the way you do," Mandie said. "And when you get to be a world-renowned pianist or soloist, then I can say I knew you when you were just learning!" She smiled.

"Oh, Mandie, I'm not aiming for fame," Celia protested. "I only want to do this for myself and my family and friends, and maybe someday I'll be able to play or sing for a wedding or a birthday party or such."

"And we'll be right there with you when you do," Mary Lou said. "In fact, you might need Mandie or me to handle all that money you will make."

Celia frowned and said, "But I'm not doing it for money. It's just for my own enjoyment, because someday I expect to get married."

"To anyone in particular?" Mandie teased. "Like someone by the name of Robert?"

"Well, who knows?" Celia quickly replied. "But I do expect to meet other interesting young men. After all, we are still very young. I know, of course, that Joe Woodard thinks he will marry you, Mandie, but I don't think that will actually come to pass."

"You are both well ahead of me when it comes to boys. I have never had a steady fellow, so to speak," Mary Lou informed them with a little laugh. "But I'm not in a hurry to find one, either."

The registrar at the head of the room tapped the inkwell on her desk as she said loudly, "Young ladies, may I have your attention please?" She waited a moment for the conversations to cease and then said, "If you have no questions regarding your schedules, you are dismissed. You may go by your classrooms, where you will find instructors available to answer any questions you may have about their classes. As you already know, you will report for chapel services every school day after breakfast, and then you will be off to your first class immediately thereafter. Thank you."

Everyone got up to leave the chapel.

Mandie, Celia, and Mary Lou paused just outside the doorway in the hall.

"Let's go look and see what the instructor of our business class looks like," Mandie suggested to Mary Lou. Then turning to Celia she said, "And we'll go with you to see the music teacher."

The girls easily found the business classroom and were surprised to see how small it was. A tall young woman wearing spectacles was sitting behind the desk at the far end of the room. No one else was in sight.

Mandie led the way across the room toward the woman. "Are you Miss Mooney?"

"Yes, I am. What can I do for you?" the woman asked.

"I am Amanda Shaw, and this is Mary Lou Dunnigan and Celia Hamilton. Mary Lou and I have both been assigned to your business class," Mandie explained.

"Welcome." The young woman gave the girls a pleasant smile, then continued. "I hope you will enjoy learning about the world of money. It really is quite fascinating." Then looking at Celia, the young teacher said, "But, Miss Hamilton, you are not enrolled in my business class?"

"No, ma'am," Celia replied. "I am here to study music."

"How very interesting," Miss Mooney replied. "I also studied music in college, but I never seemed to fit into it. My father urged me to turn to business, which I did, and I have found I am much better at it."

After a few more minutes with Miss Mooney, Mandie told the young teacher that they had to be on their way, and the girls said good-bye and turned to leave the room.

When they got into the hall, Celia suggested that they go look at the music classroom. "So I can see who the instructor is," she said.

"Of course," Mandie replied.

"Lead the way," Mary Lou added.

The music room was much more difficult to find than the business classroom was, but they finally found it at the back of the building, way up on the top floor, more or less isolated. There was no instructor there.

Mandie teased Celia, "They've put your class all the way up here so the rest of us won't be disturbed by all those wrong notes and loud vocal exercises."

"Well, naturally they couldn't have us noisy people disturbing the entire school," Celia replied.

The main classroom was huge, and there were three smaller adjoining rooms with a piano in each. No one seemed to be around.

"I was hoping I'd get to meet the instructor," Celia said, inspecting the rooms.

After looking at all of the music rooms, the three inspected other classrooms, too. The English composition class seemed to be large. Quite a few other students were roaming around there. But the girls were surprised to find even more students crowding in to inspect the arts class.

"Hmm," Mandie said at the doorway as they looked inside the crowded room. "Seems like everyone is taking art."

"I see April Snow and Polly Cornwallis in there," Celia said.

"Some of those people may be onlookers only, like us," Mary Lou said. "So everyone here may not be an art student."

"Of course," Mandie agreed.

After looking into all the classrooms in the building, the three girls went downstairs to the sitting room on the main floor. A lot of the other girls were already there and moving about the room. Mandie found a vacant settee in the far corner and said, "Let's get that before someone else does." She headed to it, and Celia and Mary Lou followed.

As they sat down, Mandie looked across the room and saw the tall dark-haired girl who had been in line with her the first day for registration. The girl looked directly at Mandie but did not smile or speak. She seemed to be alone and was not talking with anyone else.

"Don't look now, but there's that girl I told you about who was in line with me during registration," Mandie said to Celia. "And she is staring at me."

"Oh, I know who she is," Mary Lou said. "She got the scholarship that I had applied for. The scholarship offered not only tuition, but also room and board. I didn't need it since I live so close by and don't have to stay in the dormitory."

"Oh, what is her name?" Mandie asked.

"Um, I can't remember right off, but she's not from Charleston," Mary Lou said. "I believe she's from North Carolina."

"North Carolina?" Mandie repeated in surprise. "So am I. I wonder where in North Carolina she's from?"

"I don't know, but I can try to find out for you if you really want to know," Mary Lou promised. "I have spoken a few words with her a couple of times and could ask her next time I run into her."

"If you think of it, all right, but don't go to any trouble to find out," Mandie replied. "Sooner or later I'm sure I'll meet her in a class or somewhere, and I can talk to her then."

"Are you staying for the noon meal today?" Celia asked Mary Lou.

"No. I was just going to say that since we are free to go for the rest of the day, I should get home," Mary Lou replied.

"I just remembered something," Mandie said suddenly. "Mr. Ryland is probably out there waiting for us to give him our schedule so he'll know when we would be free to go somewhere."

"Oh, I had already forgotten. Let's walk outside and see if he's there," Celia said, rising as the others joined her.

"I'll go with you," Mary Lou said.

The three hurried out to the road where the carriages were parked, and sure enough, Mr. Ryland was there with their carriage. When he saw them coming, he stepped down from his seat with his hat in his hand.

"Oh, Mr. Ryland, I'm sorry we forgot that you would be

waiting," Mandie apologized. "We've got our schedules, and I don't think we'll be needing the carriage in the mornings."

"Are you sure, young lady?" Mr. Ryland asked. "The carriage is yours, and I am your driver whenever you would like to use it."

Mandie had a sudden idea. She turned to Mary Lou and asked, "Are you leaving now to go home?"

"Yes, I think I'd better," Mary Lou replied.

Turning back to Mr. Ryland, Mandie said, "You could take Mary Lou home since we don't need the carriage today." Then she showed Mr. Ryland their schedule of classes, all of which were before noon. "So you see, we won't be needing the carriage in the mornings."

"Then I will be back after noon tomorrow to check with you again," Mr. Ryland said. "But right now I would be glad to give your friend a ride home, if she needs it."

"Go ahead, Mary Lou, and let Mr. Ryland take you home," Mandie urged. "It will save you having to hire a carriage."

Mary Lou stepped up into the carriage and said, "Thank you, Mandie. Let's all meet in chapel tomorrow morning."

"Yes, that sounds perfect." Mandie and Celia waved to Mary Lou as Mr. Ryland drove the carriage down the street.

Then the two girls turned and hurried back toward the college to get to the dining hall in time for the noon meal.

chapter 5

The next day everything seemed to settle down into a routine. Mandie and Celia went to breakfast in the dining hall and then to chapel, where they found Mary Lou waiting for them. She had saved two seats next to her.

Mary Lou whispered to Mandie, "I just spoke with the girl you asked about. Her name is Grace Wilson, and she is studying art, in preparation for a career as a dress designer. She is from Raleigh, North Carolina."

"That's way upstate; nowhere near where I come from in Macon County," Mandie replied. "And she is going to be a dress designer. That's probably why all her clothes look unfamiliar from anything I've seen in the stores; she must make them herself."

"Probably. I'm sure it is great practice," Mary Lou replied.

Celia leaned across Mandie to speak to Mary Lou. "Mandie and I are in the first class of English composition. Is that the one you are in?"

"Yes, and since it's required of all the students, and there are only three classes per day, I imagine it will be a huge class," Mary Lou replied.

Reverend Coggins, the school's minister, stepped up onto the stage, tapped lightly on the pulpit, cleared his voice, and loudly said, "Good morning, young ladies."

"Good morning," came the loud reply from the entire audience.

Mandie and her friends straightened up and listened as he discussed the Ten Commandments and how they would apply in this school. The young, handsome reverend spoke with a loud, clear voice that held the attention of every girl in the room.

As soon as they were dismissed, Celia whispered to Mandie, "I do believe the reverend is from Virginia, my home state. Did you hear his accent? It's just like mine!"

Mandie grinned at her and said, "I wonder if he is single?"

"Oh, Mandie," Celia replied, blushing in spite of herself.

Mary Lou had overheard Mandie's comment and said to her friends, "I hear that he is single and lives in the small house way back there in the school's backyard." Then she looked directly at Celia and added, "And I hear his mother lives with him."

"Oh, come on, we have a class to get to," Celia said, pushing her way through the crowd.

The mornings were filled with three different classes before the noonday meal. No classes were scheduled in the afternoons because of the heat and humidity. The girls were expected to stay in their rooms and study then.

Mandie and Celia walked with Mary Lou again after classes to where Mr. Ryland was waiting with the carriage.

"Mr. Ryland, we are not going anywhere this afternoon," Mandie told the man. "However, if you would please take Mary Lou home again today, we would appreciate it."

"Yes, miss. My pleasure," Mr. Ryland replied.

"Mandie, you can't keep doing this," Mary Lou protested. "I am supposed to get a hired hack to go home when my father is not coming for me."

"I believe Mr. Ryland goes home near where you live, so it's not really out of his way," Mandie said, then spoke to Mr. Ryland. "Isn't that right?"

"Yes, miss, I go down the very street where the miss lives on my way home each day," Mr. Ryland replied.

"Well, all right, Mandie. I really appreciate the ride," Mary Lou told her. "However, my mother has already said you and Celia must come to our house one Saturday and spend the day with us."

"Oh, that would be nice," Mandie said.

Turning to Celia, Mary Lou added, "And I have a player piano."

Celia's eyes opened wide. "You really do?"

"Yes. My great-aunt gave it to me last year. And I have lots of rolls of music to play on it."

"I would really love to come to see you, Mary Lou, and see that piano," Celia said.

"Well, what about next Saturday?" Mandie asked Mary Lou.

"Would that be suitable for your mother?"

"I'm sure it would be, but I'll ask anyway and let you know tomorrow," Mary Lou promised.

As Mr. Ryland drove the carriage off, another carriage came up and stopped in the parking space. Mandie saw the British fellow, George Stuart, and a dark-haired young man step down to the street.

Mandie looked at George Stuart just as he looked at her. She blushed and told Celia, "Come on, let's hurry." She started walking back toward the college. The two fellows were following, and she heard George say, "I'm sorry that I cannot speak to the young lady, because I have not been properly introduced."

The other fellow laughed and asked, "Since when does that matter?"

Mandie felt her face turn red, and she urged Celia on toward their dormitory, where she knew young men were not allowed.

"We'd better get ready to go to the dining room," Celia remarked.

"We have a few minutes, I believe. Let's see if we have any mail," Mandie replied. She walked over to the alcove where rows of mailboxes were, though she wasn't really expecting any mail.

Both girls twirled the combination knobs on their individual boxes and both were surprised to find mail inside.

Quickly pulling out a large envelope, Mandie said, "Oh, I have a letter from my mother."

"So do I." Celia removed a smaller white envelope from her box.

"Let's go up to our room to read these," Mandie said, leading the way up the marble steps.

Mandie was examining the envelope instead of watching where she was going, causing her to nearly collide with another girl at the top of the stairs.

"Oh, I'm so sorry!" Mandie exclaimed as she quickly stepped out of the way of the girl. She had seen the girl several times in the hallways, but the girl gathered up her long skirts, turned up her nose, and quickly continued down the stairwell.

"Well!" Mandie was dumbfounded as she stood watching the girl walk away. "Just who does she think she is?"

"Mandie," Celia said, "that was just one of several incidents of that kind that has happened at this college."

"What do you mean, Celia?"

"Maybe you've been too busy to notice, but in my opinion, this college seems to be full of snobs. No one has spoken to me yet, or to you, either, that I know of," Celia explained.

Mandie looked at her friend with a frown. "You're right, I haven't noticed," she said. "But come to think of it, I guess the girls here have not been friendly at all."

As the two continued down the hallway toward their room, Celia said, "I suppose I haven't been friendly, either. I haven't really tried to talk to any of them, except the girls we knew back at the Misses Heathwood's School."

As Mandie opened the door to their room she said, "Let's make it a point to speak to everyone we come in contact with and see what happens." She went over to sit in one of the big chairs, and Celia dropped into the other one.

Celia pulled her mother's letter out of the envelope and quickly scanned it. "Mother says she probably won't be able to come back here until Thanksgiving, when she'll come to get me and ride home with me for the holiday."

Mandie quickly read her letter from her mother. "My mother also expects me home for Thanksgiving, and Grandmother is planning to be at our house then." Mandie glanced at the sealed letter that had come inside the envelope from her mother. The return address was that of a young fellow she had met in Ireland the previous summer when her grandmother had taken her and several friends on a trip around Europe. Adrian Nolan was very good-looking, with light brown hair and blue eyes. He was also a very interesting young fellow. And he had told Mandie that he might just fall in love with her.

The memories made her blush, and she quickly put the letter back into the larger envelope without opening it. She wanted a chance to do that in private.

Mandie went over to her bureau and dropped the big envelope into the top drawer, then went to freshen up.

In the dining hall Mandie and Celia found it crowded, and after filling their trays, they located two seats between girls they did not know. When they sat down, Mandie looked at the one next to her and smiled. The girl immediately picked up her tray and walked away.

The girl next to Celia glanced at Celia and Mandie, then

quickly turned back to the girl on her other side and continued their conversation.

"Oh well," Mandie whispered to Celia as they sat down and began their meal.

Mandie finally realized she and Celia were being ignored by all the other girls, and she didn't know why. She and Celia could not come up with any reason they would be disliked by all the girls at the college, so they kept smiling at everyone, hoping one day someone would return the smile.

They noticed that April Snow and Polly Cornwallis seemed to be together a lot with the other girls.

Mandie and Celia discussed the problem with Mary Lou, who was surprised to hear that Mandie and Celia were having problems with the other girls. Mary Lou said the other girls had always been friendly with her. She promised to help Mandie and Celia find out the reason for the other girls' snobbery.

That Saturday Mandie and Celia went to visit Mary Lou. The Dunnigans lived in a huge white house with stained glass in the window trim and the double front door. A wide veranda ran around the house. On it sat numerous rocking chairs, a swing fastened to the ceiling, and dozens of potted plants. Above the tall three stories was an attic with windows in it. Mary Lou was waiting on the porch.

"Oh, Mary Lou, I love your house!" Mandie exlaimed to Mary Lou as Mr. Ryland stopped the carriage in front of it. "It's so different from other houses I've seen here in Charleston."

"Thank you," Mary Lou replied, stepping down from the front

porch. "My great-great-grandfather built it, so it's been in the family quite a long time. Come on, my mother and father are waiting at the door."

Mr. and Mrs. Dunnigan were both as friendly as Mary Lou, who was their only child. Then Mrs. Dunnigan said she must see to the noon meal, and Mr. Dunnigan left to go to his office in the back of the house.

Mary Lou led the other girls to a parlor, which was full of beautiful antiques. Mandie kept glancing around for the piano Mary Lou had told them about, but it was nowhere to be seen. Finally Celia could wait no longer. "Where is your piano, Mary Lou?"

Mary Lou laughed and said, "Come on. It's in the back room where it won't distract visitors in the parlor."

Mary Lou showed them the many paper rolls with perforations, which she placed one at a time on the roller in the front of the piano, and then she pumped the pedal with her foot so the rolls would turn and play music. Each roll played a different song.

"Oh, please, you must let me try it!" Celia was excited as she watched the piano keys move up and down without anyone even touching them.

Celia found the piano difficult to operate at first, as the pedals required some strength to push down, but she soon had it going. Her paper roll was playing "Standing on the Promises," and Mandie and Mary Lou began singing and clapping their hands. "Standing on the promises of Christ my King, through eternal ages let His praises ring; Glory in the highest, I will shout and sing, standing on the promises of God."

Celia managed to join in with the chorus without missing a beat. "Standing, standing, standing on the promises of God, my Saviour, standing, standing, I'm standing on the promises of God."

As the roll ended, all three girls were breathing heavily.

"That was wonderful!" Celia exclaimed.

"I have a lot more rolls; do you want to play more?" Mary Lou asked.

"Oh yes," Celia replied.

Celia played while Mandie and Mary Lou sang until Mrs. Dunnigan called them to the table for the noon meal.

Mr. Ryland returned at four o'clock to take Mandie and Celia back to the college. "We have to go now, Mrs. Dunnigan," Mandie told her friend's mother. "We have enjoyed the visit so much. I hope someday y'all will be able to come to my home in North Carolina for a visit."

"We'll certainly try," Mrs. Dunnigan replied. "It has been a wonderful day for us, also. Since Mary Lou has no brothers or sisters, it gets rather quiet around here sometimes."

"I thank you also for such a wonderful time," Celia said. "Maybe y'all can come up to Virginia to visit with my mother and me when school is out."

Mrs. Dunnigan replied, "Yes, dear, we'll see about that."

Mary Lou followed them outside and said, "I'll see y'all Monday."

"Will you not be at church tomorrow?" Mandie asked, stepping up to the carriage seat.

"Yes, we go to church every time the doors open, but we don't go to the church near the college," Mary Lou explained. "It's too far from here. And we've belonged to our little church down the street for as long as I can remember. So I'll see you both on Monday."

Saturday visits to Mary Lou's house almost turned into a regular routine, but Mandie didn't want to impose on the good people for a meal every week, so sometimes they went to see Mary Lou after the noon meal.

At the college, Mandie and Celia gave up on trying to befriend any of the other girls and more or less stayed to themselves when it was possible. Studies were much harder than they had been used to back home at the Misses Heathwood's School for Girls, and they had to spend more time studying.

Mandie and Celia went to the art shop where Mrs. Taft had ordered the painting of a cat for Mandie a couple of weeks earlier. Mandie was excited with the work Victoria had done. Looking at the painting, it could have been Snowball himself, though the artist had never even seen him before. Mandie hung the painting by her bed where she could see it every day.

It surprised Mandie when one day Celia said to her, "You know, I'm still uncomfortable being around these snobbish girls. They are making me miserable, and I just don't trust them."

"I thought you had just given up on it, like I have."

"No," Celia groaned. "I'll never give up on anything like that. These girls are all so ill-mannered."

"Well, I don't know what we can do about it," Mandie said sadly.

"I don't know, either, but I hope and pray the situation will straighten itself out," Celia said. "In the meantime, I am most uncomfortable in the presence of these girls here."

The next Saturday while at Mary Lou's house, Mandie mentioned the situation to Mrs. Dunnigan. "We'd be so happy at the school if the girls would only act like young ladies."

"Oh dear, I can't believe the situation is so bad," Mrs. Dunnigan replied. "Mary Lou has never said anything about the snobbery of the other girls, so I assume she is not experiencing the same ill will that you girls seem to have discovered."

Suddenly Mrs. Dunnigan remembered something. "Did you know the school is renting out its boardinghouse to a lady who will take in boarders? The college doesn't need the boardinghouse this year, and Mrs. Thomason is renting to ladies only. Maybe you two—"

Mandie quickly interrupted. "Maybe we could move into the boardinghouse?" She looked excitedly at Celia.

"Do you think the school would allow it?" Celia asked.

"I'm sure that would not be a problem. The main question is whether your parents would allow it," Mrs. Dunnigan said. "I happen to know Mrs. Thomason very well and would trust her with my own daughter."

"Exactly where is this boardinghouse? Is it the one those young men in the schoolyard were talking about being haunted?" Celia asked, looking at Mrs. Dunnigan and then at Mandie.

"It's just on the next street from here," Mrs. Dunnigan told the girls. "In fact, when the vines are not too thick, we can go out in our backyard and see the backyard of the boardinghouse. Would you like me to get some information from Mrs. Thomason to give your parents?"

"Oh yes, ma'am," Mandie quickly replied.

"I'm not sure my mother would go along with this, but I could certainly find out," Celia remarked.

"Would you like to walk around to the house?" Mary Lou asked. "I can take you there."

The girls nodded their heads in interest, and the three walked down the street and around the block. The house was huge with a side gate opening into the yard by the front porch, which was also on the side, with another huge porch above it.

"There's no one there yet," Mary Lou explained as she pushed open the gate and went inside the yard. Since the house was locked, they could only look at the outside.

"And this is the house that is supposed to be haunted?" Mandie asked.

"Yes." Mary Lou laughed. "That's what some people believe, but I don't think there is such a thing as a ghost."

Mandie glanced at Celia, who was frowning as she stared at the huge old house. "Maybe we could solve the mystery of the ghost, Celia!" She laughed.

"It's probably just some tale someone made up to scare people," Celia said.

"That's what my parents and I think, also," Mary Lou agreed.

"I suppose we could talk to Mrs. Thomason and see if she has a room for us," Mandie decided. "And of course it would probably take some doing to get my mother to agree for me to move in here. And I would certainly have to do it without letting my grandmother know before it was done."

"All right, it's agreeable with me, Mandie," Celia said. "We can try."

As the girls returned to the Dunnigans' house, Mandie said, "At least we have the carriage to take us back and forth to school. I guess Grandmother was right to insist on it after all." She laughed.

The next week Mrs. Dunnigan had Mrs. Thomason come to her house and meet the girls and discuss her plans for the house. Mrs. Thomason was an older woman, and Mandie liked her immediately.

"Now, I wouldn't want you young ladies moving in one day and out the next if someone got to talking about ghosts in the house," Mrs. Thomason warned them.

"I don't think we could do that anyway. Once we give up our room at the dormitory we'll probably have to stay in your house for the rest of the year," Mandie explained.

"Well, I insist you both write your parents to make sure they are in agreement with this plan," Mrs. Thomason said. "I have a few ladies already living in the house, but I definitely have more rooms vacant."

After returning to the college that afternoon, Mandie and Celia both sat down and wrote letters to their parents, trying to explain the situation at the college with the girls, and giving them references Mrs. Thomason supplied.

"I'm not very hopeful that my mother will agree to this," Celia said with a sigh as she folded the letter.

"I'm hoping Uncle John will come to my aid with my mother," Mandie said. "As long as my grandmother doesn't find out about it, I may be able to convince him."

"It's nice that your uncle John married your mother after your father died, and she is not all alone like my mother," Celia said.

"I know," Mandie replied. "But your father's sister, Rebecca, moved into your house to be with your mother, so she is not exactly alone."

"No, not exactly. And I do love my aunt Rebecca so much," Celia said.

Mandie suddenly remembered the letter her mother had sent her from the young man in Europe. Mandie had put it in her bureau unopened. Now she was itching to get an opportunity to do so without Celia around. She would have to figure out how she could do that. Maybe while Celia was taking a bath? Great idea; that's when she would open it.

———

That night Mandie urged Celia to take her bath first, that she didn't mind waiting. When Celia finally went into the bathroom and Mandie could hear the water running, she hurried over to the bureau and retrieved the letter.

Quickly breaking the seal and removing the letter from the

envelope, Mandie unfolded the linen paper and read:

My dearest Amanda,

 I have missed you since you went back home. I have no eyes for any other young lady. My heart is deflated. I long for the day when I will again be in the presence of my dear Amanda. Please come back to Ireland. And please do me the honor of replying to my letter. I await your reply.

Longingly,

Adrian

Mandie quickly refolded the sheet of paper, placed it back into the envelope, and returned it to the bureau drawer. She sat down in the big chair and thought about this young fellow. She was not sure she should answer the letter and get into correspondence with him. After all, he was so far away, and they were both so young.

Celia came out of the bathroom in her robe. "Your turn, Mandie."

Mandie took her time in the bath, and after the girls had gone to bed for the night, Mandie lay awake for several hours, thinking about the boardinghouse and hoping her uncle John would be in favor of it. When she had written to tell her mother and him about the rude girls at the college—girls who had been the source of much unhappiness for her and Celia—she hoped they would understand how important it was that they be moved out of the college dormitory. She believed they would.

chapter 6

Mandie and Celia both began counting the days since they had written their mothers requesting permission to move into the ladies' boardinghouse. And Mary Lou asked daily if they had heard anything.

Then one day, as they were checking their mailboxes after class, Mandie excitedly announced, "I have something from my mother!"

"So do I!" Celia remarked, withdrawing a small white envelope from her mailbox.

"Come on, let's go up to our room to read these. I can't take it standing up if it is bad news," Mandie said, hurrying ahead up the marble staircase.

In their room they threw down their books, flopped into the two big chairs, and tore open the envelopes.

Mandie read the letter to herself.

Dearest daughter,

I am sorry things are not working out for you with the other girls there at the college. We could possibly talk about a transfer to another school when you come home for Thanksgiving. In the meantime, I have discussed the situation with your uncle John, and he definitely agrees that something must be done. Of course, we believe that the only alternative right now is for you and Celia to move into the boarding-house. We have contacted Mrs. Thomason and checked everything out, and we feel we can trust you girls to live there. Celia's mother is in complete agreement with us.

We have made arrangements financially with Mrs. Thomason for both of you girls, and you are free to move whenever you have time.

We have also notified the college that you girls will be moving into the boardinghouse and will relinquish your room in the dormitory as soon as this can be accomplished.

We are trusting your carriage driver, Mr. Ryland, to accomplish the move for you, and also to drive you girls back and forth to classes each day.

Please let us know the minute you begin the move. I certainly wish the telegraph company would hurry up and get the wires into town so we can have telephone service. They are working on it right now.

With all my love always,
Mother

Celia had read her own letter by the time Mandie finished, and they excitedly embraced each other and danced around the room.

"I'm so happy!" Mandie said, laughing.

"So am I!" Celia replied, dancing around the room.

"I can hardly wait until morning, when we can let Mary Lou know of the good news!" Mandie said.

The next morning Mandie and Celia stood at the chapel doors, watching for Mary Lou, and when she arrived both of them hugged her.

"You got permission?" Mary Lou guessed as she freed herself from the hugs.

Both girls nodded and Mary Lou said, "I'm so excited! Let's get things moving this afternoon."

"I think we need to go see Mrs. Thomason this afternoon and find out when it's convenient for her for us to move into her boardinghouse," Mandie said.

"First of all, I think we need to go look at the room we'll be getting so we'll know how to arrange our things. We haven't even seen a room in her house yet," Celia reminded Mandie.

"You're right," Mandie agreed. "Now we just have to get through this day's classes." She led the way into the chapel.

When classes were finished for the day, Mary Lou suggested that they all go to her house and eat their noon meal, then go around to see Mrs. Thomason.

Mr. Ryland was waiting at the carriage parking, and he smiled at them as he said, "I have instructions from both of your mothers to move you young ladies into the boardinghouse."

"Yes, sir," Mandie and Celia said together.

"But we have to go see Mrs. Thomason first," Mandie

explained, "so if you could please take us to Mary Lou's house, we'll eat there, and then we'll walk around to see Mrs. Thomason while you go home for your noon meal."

"Yes, young lady," Mr. Ryland agreed as he helped the three into the carriage.

Mrs. Dunnigan already had the noon meal waiting for Mary Lou, and she quickly added two plates for Mandie and Celia. As soon as they entered the house, they excitedly told Mary Lou's mother the news.

"I'm so happy for you young ladies," she said as they all sat down at the table.

Mr. Dunnigan, who was also present for the noon meal, offered any help he could provide for the move.

"Thank you, Mr. Dunnigan," Mandie told him. "Mr. Ryland has already been contacted by my mother to move us, but he could probably use some help." She turned to grin at Celia as she added, "We do have lots of things in our room."

"Just let me know when you plan to do this, and I will be of whatever assistance I can," Mr. Dunnigan promised.

The three girls hurriedly finished their food and then walked around the block to the boardinghouse.

Mrs. Thomason came to the door with a big smile on her face. "Come right in, young ladies. I have heard from both your mothers, and I have been expecting you."

Mandie was thinking that her mother really did a thorough job of planning their move, but then she realized it was probably the work of Uncle John. He was a businessman and was accustomed to such things.

Mrs. Thomason led the way into her house. "Even though we have metal bars on all the downstairs windows, I decided to put you young ladies on the second floor, where I'll feel safer about you." She led the way up the ornate staircase.

"Safer?" Mandie repeated. She glanced at Celia and smirked. "Safer from the ghost who lives here?"

Mrs. Thomason heard her and looked back at the girls. "Don't believe all those rumors. This house has been empty for a long time, and I would imagine those so-called ghosts were none other than local pranksters trying to frighten people. Anyhow, my apartment is on the first floor, and anyone coming in and out would have to get by me first." She reached the top of the stairs and turned down a wainscoted hallway. When she reached the first closed door, she stopped and opened it.

Mandie and Celia both crowded forward to look at the room. There were two single beds with canopies, several chairs, a huge wardrobe, and two bureaus. The furnishings were very similar to what they had in their room at the college.

As Mandie took in the layout of the room she said, "This is nice." She went over to the triple windows and looked out, noticing that they were on the front of the house above the roof of the huge front porch that ran around the house.

"I like this, Mrs. Thomason." Celia gave her a pleased smile.

"If there is anything that is not satisfactory, all you girls have to do is let me know," Mrs. Thomason told them as they stood in the middle of the room. "Now, when had y'all planned on moving in?"

"Just as soon as we can get back to the college and check out of there," Mandie replied. "This is going to be more like home. And it will be so nice to have Mary Lou just around the corner."

Mr. Ryland drove Mandie, Celia, and Mary Lou back to the college, and they immediately went to the office. Things seemed to drag there as it took quite some time to fill out papers, change their status to day students, have their room freed for someone else, and quickly pack trunks.

Mr. Ryland returned with a hired hack, which he had employed to carry the baggage. After everything was loaded up, the girls climbed back into the carriage, and Mr. Ryland drove them back to the boardinghouse, where Mrs. Thomason helped them get settled in.

As they hung up the last of their clothes in the wardrobe, Mrs. Thomason told them about the schedule for meals. "Supper is usually at six, but since I only have you ladies plus two others right now, we can be flexible. But when the house is filled up, we will get on a strict routine."

"Why don't y'all come home with me and eat supper with us tonight?" Mary Lou asked.

"Your mother has already fed us one meal today. We can't impose on her hospitality," Mandie said.

"Hospitality? You are doing us a favor when you visit with us," Mary Lou informed her. "Now, let's go back to my house."

Mandie and Celia looked at each other and smiled. Then

Mandie said, "Well, all right, but we can't make this a habit."

"Then I will not wait on supper tonight for you ladies," Mrs. Thomason told them. "But before you leave, let's go down to my office so I can give you some keys. I keep the doors locked day and night, so you should never go anywhere without your key."

On the main floor, Mrs. Thomason showed them into a small office where another lady, younger and prettier, was busy at a desk. Mrs. Thomason introduced the girls to her. "This is Miss Flora. She handles the business part of the house. And Miss Flora, this is Miss Amanda Shaw and Miss Celia Hamilton. They need keys."

"I'm sure you girls will like it here." Miss Flora seemed cheerful as she took two keys out of the desk drawer.

"Thank you," Mandie and Celia replied.

"Now, the same key fits both the front and back doors," Miss Flora explained to the girls.

"Of course, we hope you never have to use the back door," Mrs. Thomason said as she led the way back to the front hallway. "We leave a lamp burning all night in here, and there is also one in the hallway at the top of each floor's stairway." She walked over to a table and pointed to the book lying open on it. "This is a sign-in book. Signing in and out is the only strict rule we have. For security reasons, we must know when you go and come, and both your mothers asked that we be sure to enforce that rule."

"I agree with you, Mrs. Thomason," Mandie said, picking up the pen to sign her name and the time on the next line in the book. Celia quickly added hers, also.

"Now, you girls have a nice time at the Dunnigans' tonight," Mrs. Thomason told them as they went out the front door.

"We won't be very late tonight. I'm just plain tired out," Mandie told Mrs. Thomason.

But time flew at the Dunnigans'. After a hearty supper, the three girls played the piano while discussing the effects Mandie and Celia's moving out of the dormitory would have on the snobbish girls at the college. But it wasn't long until the conversation got around to the rumor that the boardinghouse was haunted.

"Those are all silly tales the boys have made up just to frighten the girls," Mary Lou assured Mandie and Celia. "Up until Mrs. Thomason got in there, the house stood empty, so it was inviting to tale-toters."

"But now people can't get into the house anymore, since Mrs. Thomason has people living there," Mandie said.

"Anyhow, I do hope it's not really haunted," Celia said with a little sigh. "Because if it is, Mandie will have us all involved in solving the mystery."

"Do you suppose Mrs. Thomason will be able to keep renting the house for a while?" Mandie asked.

"She told my mother she had signed a five-year lease on it, so she will be there at least that long," Mary Lou explained. "And that's longer than y'all will need to rent a room from her, since you'll be graduated and gone."

"Thank goodness!" Mandie exclaimed. "My mother mentioned in her letter to me that we might consider changing colleges, and I didn't want to have to do that."

"No, I don't want you to do that!" Mary Lou quickly said, her face suddenly full of worry.

"I'll see what my mother has to say when I go home for Thanksgiving," Mandie said.

Mandie and Celia decided they should return to the boardinghouse by eight o'clock in order to have plenty of time to get ready for bed. It was not yet dark outside, but Mr. Dunnigan and Mary Lou walked with them to the boardinghouse.

"I'm sorry I didn't get to help you young ladies move, but it happened so suddenly that I didn't even know," Mr. Dunnigan said as they walked along the sidewalk.

"Thank you anyhow, sir," Mandie replied, "but we decided the quicker we could get out of that dormitory, the better."

"I hope you all will enjoy living with Mrs. Thomason. She's a fine lady," Mr. Dunnigan said.

When they arrived at the boardinghouse, Mr. Dunnigan and Mary Lou waited until Mandie and Celia had unlocked the front door, gone inside, and locked it again before they left.

They hurried up to their room and found someone had turned down their beds for the night and laid out soap and towels in their private bathroom.

"I think I could just collapse right into bed without undressing, I'm so tired," Mandie said with a loud groan as she quickly began undressing.

"So could I," Celia agreed.

Crawling into bed, it wasn't long before the two girls were fast asleep.

Mandie was dreaming but suddenly woke up. What had awakened her? Without moving, she gazed about the nearly pitch-black room. Her heart was pounding as she tried to calm her breathing.

Then she noticed that Celia seemed to be awake, also.

"Celia," she said softly but with alarm in her voice.

"Yes," Celia replied in an unsteady voice. "Did you hear that?"

"No. What?" Mandie asked, still not moving.

Then there was a loud scratching sound coming from across the darkness in the room. Celia immediately jumped out of her bed and into bed with Mandie.

"Mandie! What is that?" she whispered as she pulled the cover up around her.

Mandie tried to calm herself. She took a deep breath and said, "I heard it, but I don't know what it is."

Then the noise was repeated. Both girls dived under the covers.

After a few moments Mandie ventured out of the cover to look around again. She couldn't see anything, but she remembered a lamp sitting on a table near the bed. She fumbled in the darkness to find the switch and turn it on. The room was illuminated and there was nothing or no one in sight. She fell back onto her pillow as Celia finally ventured out of the covers to look around.

The two girls held their breath, waiting to see if the noise was repeated. After a few minutes of sitting in total silence,

Mandie said, "Whatever it was, it's gone."

The adjoining bathroom door was open, and Mandie got the nerve to get up and go look inside the bathroom. She crept slowly to the door and held her breath as she peered around the open door. There was no one inside. She released a big sigh as she jumped back into bed.

"Nothing there," she declared.

"I know I heard something, Mandie. I didn't imagine it. Whatever it was woke me up," Celia said.

"Let's pull the shades down and leave the light on for the rest of the night," Mandie said, throwing back the counterpane. She looked at the clock on the mantelpiece. It was twenty minutes after two.

"All right, but can I sleep with you, Mandie?" Celia asked, slowly getting out of bed to help pull down the shades.

"Of course," Mandie said. "I think it would have been better to have one big bed anyhow in a strange place like this."

They jumped back into Mandie's bed and pulled the covers up to their chins. Celia was soon asleep, but Mandie stayed awake for a long time, wondering what the noise had been and if it would happen again. Her eyelids grew heavy and she finally drifted off to sleep.

A long time later Celia woke with a start, looked at Mandie, who was still asleep, and then saw that it was eight o'clock and daylight was creeping in around the edges of the shades.

"Mandie," Celia said, reaching to shake her. "We need to get up for breakfast."

Mandie instantly sat up, rubbing her eyes. "Yes, it must be time for breakfast. I smell the coffee." She threw back the covers and sat up on the side of the bed and yawned.

Celia sat up on her side of the bed, rubbed her eyes, and said, "Whatever that was last night, it certainly ruined my night."

Mandie slipped out of bed and quickly raised the shades. The sunlight was already bright. She looked out the windows and couldn't see anyone down in the street. Everything seemed to be quiet.

Going back to flop down on the bed, she yawned and asked, "Do you suppose that was the ghost making that noise?"

"I thought we had decided there was no such thing as a ghost," Celia replied, looking directly at Mandie.

Just then there was a knock at the door, causing both of them to jump. The knock was repeated a few seconds later, and then a voice outside said, "Breakfast is ready."

Mandie hurried across the room and opened the door to a tall girl in a uniform. The girl smiled and said, "I know y'all are new and don't have a schedule yet, but breakfast is waiting."

"Oh, thank you, we'll be down as soon as we get dressed," Mandie replied.

The girl went on down the hall, and Mandie closed the door.

Mandie and Celia quickly dressed and followed the smell of coffee downstairs to the dining room.

There was a glassed-in room at the back of the house, with windows on three sides, filled with chairs and tables. On the far wall was an enormous amount of food on a long table. No one else was in the room.

The girls paused at the door and Mandie said, "What do you think we're supposed to do? Go in there and eat with no one else around? Or wait to be served?"

Her question was answered as the girl who had awakened them came in through the door at the other side of the room and said, "Help yourselves, and I will bring the coffee to the table for you." She moved toward the display of cups and saucers.

Mandie and Celia took plates from the stack and filled them with scrambled eggs, bacon, and biscuits. They sat down near a window where they could look outside, and soon the girl brought their coffee.

"My name is Sadie. I work in the kitchen and the dining room and do the wake-up calls," the girl said.

"You seem to have an awful lot of food over there," Mandie remarked. "I thought there was only us plus two other boarders."

"Last night people started arriving in groups. I was up most of the night answering the door," Sadie explained. She walked across the room to greet two older women who were coming in.

Mandie looked at Celia and asked, "Do you suppose the noise we heard could have been the sound of some of those people arriving last night?"

Celia thought about that for a moment as she held her fork. "But what could they have been doing to make that odd noise?"

Mandie paused and set her cup down. "I don't know, but if we think about it long enough we might find the answer."

"Are we going to tell Mary Lou about it?" Celia asked.

"Of course," Mandie replied, sipping from her coffee cup. "Maybe she will have some ideas about what it could have been."

They hurriedly finished breakfast, then went back to their room to freshen up before going to Mary Lou's.

As she brushed her hair, Celia asked, "Mandie, do you think that noise could have been a ghost, just like those boys were talking about?"

Mandie looked at her as she retied her sash and said, "Oh, Celia, it was just talk before. You know there is no such thing as a ghost."

"Well, whatever it was, it was spooky," Celia declared.

"Don't you think we ought to write a note to our mothers and tell them we have moved?" Mandie asked, going to look in a drawer for her envelopes and paper.

"You are right," Celia agreed, getting her paper out. "We were supposed to let them know when we started moving, so they will be surprised to find out that it's already happened!"

They both wrote quick notes saying they had moved and they would write more later.

Mandie suddenly remembered the letter from Adrian. She must write him and at least give him her new address so he wouldn't keep writing to her house for her mother to notice.

Then Mandie thought of something else.

"Celia, writing letters reminds me. Sooner or later I will have to write and tell Grandmother that I have moved," she said. "And she is not going to like that one bit."

"You're right," Celia agreed.

But since Mandie's mother had arranged for Mandie to move out of the dormitory, her grandmother couldn't fuss too much. After all, Elizabeth Shaw was her mother, and Mrs. Taft was only her grandmother.

All the same, she dreaded the time when Mrs. Taft would learn about this move. It promised to be a very upsetting scene.

c h a p t e r 7

After spending the day with the Dunnigans, Mandie and Celia returned to their room and prepared their clothes for church with the Dunnigans the next day. While Celia was in the bathroom, Mandie quickly wrote a note to Adrian, put it in an envelope, and sealed it. She would give it to Miss Flora to mail for her. Now he would not have to write to her home where her mother would notice the letters. Somehow or other she wanted to keep this correspondence all private.

The members of the Dunnigans' church welcomed the girls, and Mandie and Celia decided they would continue to attend there rather than the church near the college.

Then Monday came and Mandie was not anxious to go to her classes, because by then word would have gotten around that she and Celia had moved into the boardinghouse.

As Mr. Ryland drew the carriage up in the parking space, Mandie saw another carriage discharging passengers—some of the girls who had snubbed them. She also noticed that George

Stuart was in the carriage with the other fellow who seemed to be his friend.

George looked directly at Mandie, smiled, and turned to his friend and said loudly, "Would you believe that those two young ladies have moved into the boardinghouse with the ghost now?"

His friend replied, "I do hope the ghosts are not dangerous."

Mandie didn't even look at them as she muttered loud enough for them to hear, "I do believe those two grown men are afraid of such things as ghosts." She quickly walked down the drive with Celia and Mary Lou and didn't look back, but she heard the two young fellows laugh loudly.

The three didn't slow down until they came to the chapel doors, which were standing open for the morning service. They quickly went inside and took seats toward the back. Mandie noticed several of the girls there turned their heads to look at her, then quickly looked away. She straightened her shoulders, tilted her chin, and sat down. She didn't have to look at them.

As the days went by, the other girls seemed to notice Mandie and Celia less and less; Mandie felt better by just ignoring them all.

Then one day Mandie received a note from the office right before dismissal time from classes. Mandie quickly read, *Your grandmother has asked that we let you know she is waiting to speak to you in the main sitting room. Please meet her after your last class of the day.*

"Oh no!" Mandie exclaimed. She told Celia and Mary Lou

the contents of the note, then sighed. "I knew she would be here sooner or later."

"We'll wait for you in the front reception area, Mandie," Celia replied. "And don't get too upset. We have already moved out of here, and I don't think anyone can make you move back in."

"I know, but Grandmother sure can kick up a fuss when she is displeased with something," Mandie said with a loud moan.

Mandie straightened her shoulders and walked down the hallway to the sitting room. Mrs. Taft was sitting by a window and didn't see her come in until Mandie stood directly before her.

"Hello, Grandmother," Mandie greeted, trying her best to put on a good smile.

Mrs. Taft looked up at Mandie and replied, "Oh, hello, Amanda. Would you sit down, please."

As Mandie sat in the chair opposite her grandmother, Mrs. Taft said, "I've come down here to discuss the matter of your moving out of the dormitory. Your mother told me what has happened, and I must say that you don't have to leave the dormitory because of some rude, ill-mannered girls. Your grandfather's family are big benefactors of this school. Over the years they have donated literally millions of dollars." She paused to let that sink in.

"Well, that doesn't change some people's attitudes. I have never felt comfortable here, so under the circumstances, I thought it was best I move out of the dormitory. Celia and I are happy now in Mrs. Thomason's boardinghouse."

"But you'll never meet the right people living in such a place. I'm surprised that your mother agreed to it," Mrs. Taft replied. "There are lots of eligible young men in this town, in the Citadel and the College of Charleston. Most of the girls in the college are from families high on the social register, but you will never be accepted by them living in a boardinghouse with working-class people."

"Ah, but Grandmother, you are forgetting one thing," Mandie quickly told her. "I don't belong to that class of people, and I don't want to belong to that class, either." Mrs. Taft's eyebrows rose, but Mandie continued. "My father was one-half Cherokee, which makes me one-fourth Cherokee, and I am very proud of it. I don't need to be accepted by such high-class people. I only want to be left to do my schoolwork so I can graduate and come home."

Mrs. Taft's face registered concern. "Please do some deep thinking about this, dear," she told Mandie. "And if you do change your mind and want to move back into the dormitory, rest assured your room there is ready. I have made arrangements to hold it. They will not be renting it to anyone else for at least the remainder of this year."

"You kept our room?" Mandie asked in surprise.

"Yes, it's still yours and Celia's if you decide to move back in," Mrs. Taft replied. "I did discuss that with your mother, and she agreed it would be the best thing to do." She opened her pocketbook and said, "Now, here is some mail for you that your mother gave me. Evidently Joe does not know how to address a letter to you here, nor does this other person, Adrian someone, with an Irish stamp on it." She handed Mandie four letters.

Mandie took the mail, quickly glanced at the return addresses, and put them in her notebook. "Where are you staying, Grandmother?" she asked. "Would you like to stay with us in the boardinghouse? Mrs. Thomason probably has a room empty. She said it's not full yet."

"Stay in the boardinghouse?" Mrs. Taft asked with a frown. "Why, I have a room at the hotel."

"Then would you like to come with us and meet Mrs. Thomason? You can go back to the hotel afterward," Mandie suggested.

"Yes, I suppose I should meet this woman you girls are renting a room from so I can make a report to your mother," Mrs. Taft said, rising from her chair.

"Celia and Mary Lou are waiting for me in the reception room," Mandie said, leading the way. She wondered what Celia and Mary Lou would have to say about this later.

"Celia," Mandie said as she and her grandmother walked into the reception room, "Grandmother is going to the boardinghouse with us to meet Mrs. Thomason. Mary Lou, I don't remember if you have met her, but this is my grandmother, Mrs. Taft."

"How do you do, Mrs. Taft?" Mary Lou greeted her as they all went out the front door and walked toward the carriage parking where Mr. Ryland was waiting.

"Just fine, Mary Lou, thank you," Mrs. Taft replied.

When they arrived at the boardinghouse, Mandie watched and listened as her grandmother and Mrs. Thomason became acquainted. Mrs. Taft seemed to approve of Mrs. Thomason.

Then Mandie and Celia showed Mrs. Taft their room. Since she didn't make any comments, Mandie figured her grandmother must approve of the room.

"Would you please come around the corner to my house and meet my mother, Mrs. Taft?" Mary Lou asked.

"Yes, I suppose I could," Mrs. Taft agreed.

Mr. Ryland, who was still waiting out front with the carriage, drove them around the block.

Mrs. Dunnigan welcomed Mrs. Taft and insisted she join them for the noonday meal, which was ready and waiting. Mrs. Taft agreed and sat down with them at the dining room table.

Mandie again watched her grandmother and was relieved when she seemed to immediately become friendly with Mrs. Dunnigan.

"It is so wonderful to have two other girls around, Mrs. Taft," Mrs. Dunnigan said. "I greatly enjoy the visits of Amanda and Celia. My husband works long hours a lot."

"I believe Mr. Dunnigan is a public record keeper, is he not?" Mrs. Taft asked.

"Yes, ma'am, he is," Mrs. Dunnigan replied.

Mandie looked at her grandmother and wondered how she knew this about Mr. Dunnigan. Mrs. Taft had never met the Dunnigans, as far as she knew.

"I came down here to check on the girls for both of their mothers," Mrs. Taft told her. "I'll be happy to report that the girls have found such friends as you all."

"Thank you, Mrs. Taft," Mrs. Dunnigan replied. "We are grateful for the girls' friendship."

"We would be glad to hear of anything, shall we say, out of the way, concerning the girls," Mrs. Taft said. "Since it's impossible for any of us to know things like you would here, there may be times when one of us needs to make a visit down here."

Mandie noticed Mrs. Dunnigan stiffen, and she said only, "Yes, Mrs. Taft." Evidently Mary Lou's mother did not wish to be a tale-toter. Mandie was happy about that; her grandmother could not always get everything the way she wanted it.

Mrs. Taft invited the Dunnigans and Mrs. Thomason to dine with her and the girls that night at the hotel. Mandie felt everything was working out nicely. Her grandmother had not been adamant about her moving back into the college dormitory, and she had been very friendly with Mrs. Thomason and the Dunnigans.

Finally it was time to retire for the night. Mrs. Taft stayed at the hotel, and Mandie and Celia went to their room at the boardinghouse.

Breathing a sigh of relief as she closed the door to their room, Mandie fell into one of the big chairs. "I can't believe Grandmother came all this way to check up on me. But I'm glad that she seems to like Mrs. Thomason and Mrs. Dunnigan."

Mandie reached for her notebook and took out the mail her grandmother had delivered. "At last, I can see what Joe Woodard felt it took three letters to tell me." She laughed. "And Adrian has written again."

"Robert writes to me at the college," Celia said, sitting in the other chair, "but I'll have to let him know we are living in the boardinghouse now."

Mandie nodded her head in agreement, then quickly opened Joe's letters, scanned them, and told Celia, "Joe wrote practically the same thing in all three letters. He says he has been doubling up his classes again this year. And since he couldn't remember my address at the dormitory, he felt he should just write to my house and assumed my mother would be sure to get it to me."

"Well, with all that schoolwork, I can't believe he has time to write to you—three times at that!" Celia smiled. "Evidently he doesn't want you to forget him." She laughed. "And that you are supposed to marry him when you both finish school."

"Now, Celia, you know that is only his side of the story," Mandie quickly reminded her. "I may never marry."

"When you do, I'll remind you of what you've just said," Celia said.

Mandie opened her fourth letter and quickly read it. "Adrian has written practically the same thing he wrote before," Mandie said. "That shows we don't really know much about each other. He has nothing new to say." She put the letter back in the envelope and took all four of them over to her bureau drawer.

After settling herself back in the chair, Mandie faced Celia and said, "It seems that Grandmother is not going to try to cause me any trouble about moving into this boardinghouse."

"Why would she?" Celia asked. "Your mother approved, so what could your grandmother do except accept it?"

"That is true," Mandie remarked. "She is going directly to my mother's house from here. And I suppose she'll be there for Thanksgiving, too, which is only two weeks away."

"I know. I'm actually looking forward to it," Celia said. "Aunt Rebecca has already written that she will travel down here to escort me home. Are you traveling alone when you go home?"

"Oh goodness, I had not even thought about that. Of course, it will have to be Grandmother. She won't trust me alone on a trip that far away."

But Mandie was in for a big surprise. The week before Thanksgiving she received another letter from Joe. He was coming to Charleston to take Mandie home for the holidays.

Mandie discussed his letter with Celia. "It seems that he has been doubling up classes so he could have time to come after me," she said with a frown. She wasn't sure she wanted Joe to be so possessive as to show up at her college to escort her home.

On the day that Joe arrived at Mandie's college, Mandie was

surprised to find that she looked at him proudly. Joe seemed to have settled down and become much more mature just since she had seen him in the summertime. He was wearing very stylish clothes, but he was still the same old Joe, with his big grin and twinkling brown eyes.

Mandie had had Mr. Ryland drive her and Celia to the train station to meet the train when he came in. She noticed lots of other students from her college and the boys' colleges either greeting arrivals or boarding the train themselves. Mandie again noticed many interested glances cast her way.

After finding Joe and picking up his luggage, the three traveled back to the hotel, where Mandie and Celia waited in the lobby while Joe checked in for the night. Afterward the three went into the dining room for supper.

"I would love to see your college," Joe told them, "but, Mandie, your mother asked me to bring you right back, so we'll have to get the train tomorrow. I can see your college when I bring you back after the holidays."

"You are coming back with me after Thanksgiving?" Mandie asked in surprise.

"Of course," Joe replied with a grin. "Who else is free enough to do this time-consuming chore?"

"Oh, Joe, Uncle John could have come down, or even my grandmother," Mandie replied.

Joe shook his head and said, "No, your mother didn't want your uncle John to leave her that long. And I didn't think you'd be too anxious for your dear old grandmother to travel that far again. After all, she was just here a few weeks ago, I understand. And she is not as young as she used to be." He stifled a laugh.

"I could go home by myself," Mandie said.

"Oh no, your mother would not allow that, I'm sure," Joe said. There was a brief moment of silence, and then Joe sighed deeply and said, "So you are thinking up excuses to keep me from coming down here to see what you've been up to?"

"Of course not!" Mandie countered. "I just feel like you'll go to a lot of trouble just to get me home and then back to my college." Then she added, "But I thank you."

"I thank *you*, because by doing this, I was able to talk my parents into spending Thanksgiving at your house," Joe replied, watching her closely.

Mandie's blue eyes widened as she said, "You are? I'm so glad. I thought y'all were staying home for the holidays."

"No, I changed everyone's minds," Joe said, and turning to Celia, he added, "And I'm pretty sure you are going to find your holiday plans changed, too."

"My holiday plans?" Celia asked, confused. "Aunt Rebecca is coming after me tomorrow."

"I know, but do you know where she is taking you?" Joe questioned.

"Not home?" Celia asked, looking at him and then at Mandie. "Are we going to Mandie's house instead?"

"That's right," Joe said with a wide grin. "It was a last-minute change, so your mother will be taking Mollie on to Mandie's house while your Aunt Rebecca comes after you."

Celia looked at Mandie and said, "How wonderful!"

"Yes, the Shaw house will be full. Even the New York Yankees will be coming down—Jonathan and his father," Joe explained.

Mandie frowned and asked, "Why wasn't I told about all this, Joe Woodard? Are you making this up?"

"Why would I make this up?" Joe asked. "I said it was a last-minute decision by everyone, since your mother can't travel right now," Joe explained. "And of course Uncle Ned will be there at some time."

"I hope so. I haven't seen him since I began school down here," Mandie said.

Uncle Ned was Mandie's father's old Cherokee friend. Uncle Ned had promised Jim Shaw to watch over Mandie after he had died.

"There's one other one you haven't mentioned," Joe teased her.

"Another friend that I haven't mentioned?" Mandie asked, puzzled by his question.

"Yes, the troublemaker." Joe was teasing her.

Mandie laughed and said, "Snowball! Yes, he'll be there for sure. And I've missed him, too."

"That is one spoiled cat," Joe said, shaking his head. "I'm surprised you don't have him living down here with you."

Mandie smiled and said, "You know that's impossible. However, I do have a painting of him hung up in our room."

"A painting of Snowball?" Joe asked, amused.

"We met an artist who was painting a picture of her own cat, but it looked identical to Snowball, so Mandie's grandmother got her to paint another one for Mandie," Celia explained.

"It does look like Snowball, but I can't show you because boys are not allowed past the parlor in the boardinghouse," Mandie said.

"Well, I'm glad the holidays are turning out this way," Celia said. "We'll get to see everyone, and I sure feel like some friends after all this time in this friendless college." Then she frowned as she looked at Joe and asked, "My aunt Rebecca will be coming in on the early train tomorrow morning. Does that mean we will be getting on the train with you and Mandie to go to Franklin instead of getting on the train to Virginia?"

"That's right," Joe replied. "You girls need to get your carriage driver to bring your trunks tomorrow to be put on the proper train."

"Of course," Mandie replied, and turning to Celia she said, "I'm so glad everyone is coming to my house. It will be great for everyone to catch up on things."

Later, when Joe went back to his hotel room for the night, Mandie and Celia went to their room to talk about the forthcoming holidays.

"I'm so glad to get a break from this school," Mandie said as she sat down in one of the big chairs.

"Yes, a break is good for everyone, but did you know that girl, Grace Wilson, is staying here for the holidays?" Celia asked.

Mandie sat up straighter. "You mean she is staying here at the college during the holidays? Why?"

"It seems she has no home to go to, or else she doesn't have the money to travel," Celia explained.

"Does she not have any family?" Mandie asked.

"No one seems to know, but everyone thinks she is too poor. She is here on a scholarship, remember?" Celia reminded her.

"That's too bad," Mandie said. "What will she do all during the holidays here alone?"

"She won't be alone. I understand there are two or three other girls who will be staying here because of various reasons. But you know she doesn't seem to make friends with anyone and is always by herself," Celia explained.

"I wonder why," Mandie said thoughtfully. "She probably has some kind of problem that she's keeping private."

"That's what I was thinking, too," Celia agreed. "But what could it be?"

"Since we don't live in the dormitory, I don't know much about any of the girls anymore," Mandie commented.

"Maybe she's friends with one of the girls who is staying here for Thanksgiving," Celia said.

"It's too late now to do anything about it since we are leaving in the morning, but when we come back I intend to do a little investigative work and find out a few things about her. Maybe we could help her, whatever it is."

"I've heard that she is involved in a group that makes clothes for poor children," Celia told her. "Maybe we could find out something through them."

"A group that make clothes for poor children? Not a group from this college, surely. The girls here are too high and mighty for that," Mandie said.

"No, I believe it meets somewhere in town," Celia said.

Mandie looked at Celia, laughed, and said, "Celia, you are getting to be a real busybody. How do you find out all these things?"

"Listening," Celia said, grinning. "Since we're not in all the same classes tgether, I hear a lot of talk that you don't. My music class is especially where I hear a lot of things. The girls in there seem to be friendlier than in other classes."

"And they also seem to know everyone's business, right?" Mandie added with a laugh.

"I suppose you could say that." Celia smiled. Then she stood up, stretched, and said, "I think we should be getting into bed. We have to get up awfully early tomorrow."

"You're right." Mandie also rose and started toward the wardrobe, but then she stopped and said, "You know, Celia, I haven't heard that noise at night since we first heard it. Have you?"

Celia frowned and said, "I listen every night, but I haven't heard a thing. I wonder what it was?"

"Maybe it was those people arriving here in the middle of the night," Mandie said, going to open the wardrobe and take down her nightclothes. "It seems to be the only explanation."

"I'm not sure, but I do hope we don't ever hear it again," Celia replied.

After they got into bed, Mandie lay awake thinking of Joe. It was really nice of him to come after her and to arrange for everyone to be at her house for the holidays. But he still had the idea that she was going to marry him when she finished school, and she was not sure about that.

Adrian was very interesting, and he also seemed to be very interested in her. . . .

She began to grow sleepy and finally thought to herself, *Oh, phooey to both of them.* She was going home tomorrow.

chapter 8

The Thanksgiving holidays turned out to be a glorious time with family and friends. Everyone was glad to be spending it together.

Mollie, the little Irish orphan whom they brought back from their visit to Ireland a while ago, didn't take time to get a breath between questions. She just followed Mandie around and asked her questions about Ireland and leprechauns. "Mandie, when will we go back to Ireland so I can catch a leprechaun?"

Mandie stopped, stooped down to look at her, and said, "Now, Mollie, you know there is no such thing as a leprechaun."

"Oh, but I know there are leprechauns in Ireland. Everyone there will tell you so," Mollie insisted.

"Well, whether there are or not, we are not going back to Ireland for you to hunt for one," Mandie said firmly. "Doesn't Aunt Rebecca teach you school lessons? Hasn't she taught you there is no such thing?"

"No, Aunt Rebecca has said we would go look for one

someday, but she won't say when, and I'm tired of waiting," Mollie replied.

"Then go find Aunt Rebecca and ask her just when you are going back to Ireland. I'm sorry, but I have things I have to do now."

Mandie was getting annoyed with the child for following her around. Mandie wanted time to spend with her mother and her friends.

Elizabeth came up behind Mandie in the hallway as Mandie straightened up. "I'm so glad you're home for the holidays, dear," she told Mandie as she put an arm around her. She leaned closer and whispered, "And I'm glad you got moved away from that terrible group of girls at the college."

Mandie put her arm around her mother and smiled. "Thank you, Mother, for allowing that. If Grandmother had found out about it in time, she would have tried to stop me."

"I know. She doesn't understand young people nowadays," Elizabeth confided to her daughter.

Suddenly Jonathan came down the hallway. "There you are, Mandie. Everyone is in the back parlor, and we have been waiting for you to join us."

"All right," Mandie said, giving her mother a quick squeeze and following Jonathan.

Following Jonathan back to the parlor, she found the rest of her friends waiting: Joe, Celia, and Sallie, Uncle Ned's granddaughter, who had just arrived unexpectedly with her grandparents.

As Mandie sat down near Sallie, Jonathan asked, "What are your plans for the Christmas holidays, Mandie? We've been figuring out what we can do about getting together then."

"I'll be coming home for the holidays because my mother won't be able to travel," she told them.

"Oh, that's right," Jonathan said.

They all looked at each other. Seeing as she was in mixed company, Mandie knew that it was not proper to discuss having babies, but her friends knew that was the reason her mother was unable to travel.

Joe broke the silence by saying, "I'm pretty sure my parents are planning on coming back here for the Christmas holidays, and of course I'll be with them wherever they plan to be."

"In that case, Mandie, I believe you are going to get all of us again," Jonathan told her with a big grin. "However, for the holidays in the summer, I'm expecting everyone to come to my house in New York—no excuses."

"I will have to speak to my grandparents about that," Sallie said.

"And of course I'll have to ask my mother what her plans are," Celia said.

"I suggest we all get together before Christmas and go down to Charleston and bring Mandie and Celia up here," Jonathan suggested. "I'd like to meet some of those snooty girls there. I'd tell them a thing or two." Then, glancing at Joe, he asked, "Did you meet any of them?"

Joe shook his head. "No, because we were in too big of a hurry to get here. I told Mandie I'd like to see her college when she goes back. I'll be going back with her so she has a travel companion."

"If Grandmother doesn't decide to take over and go with me," Mandie added. "But I certainly am glad we don't have to take that snobby treatment from the girls in the dormitory any longer. We moved into the boardinghouse, you know," Mandie explained to their friends.

"And it's supposed to be haunted!" Celia added, eyes wide and serious.

"A haunted boardinghouse? How did you get permission to move there?" Jonathan asked in surprise.

"Because of those girls treating us so badly," Mandie repeated.

"Does this boardinghouse really have ghosts in it? Have you seen any?" Jonathan asked.

"Oh, sure, we see one every night," Mandie teased.

"We really don't see them," Celia clarified, shaking her head. Then, with a teasing grin she added, "We hear them!"

"I think you are both joking," Jonathan said, frowning. "But I do believe in ghosts."

"You do?" Joe asked. "Have you seen one?"

"No, but some of our servants have," Jonathan replied with a solemn look. "They say our house has several ghosts living in it. It is believed they are some of the draft rioters who were killed back in 1862. Our house was built on that land a short time after the old house was torn down."

"I've never seen or heard a ghost in your house when we visited there," Mandie said.

"Is it the people who protested the draft for the Civil War?" Joe asked.

"That's right," Jonathan confirmed.

"Well, if you haven't seen or heard them, who would be a reliable source for this?" Mandie asked.

"Lots of people. When you come to visit in the summer I'll introduce you to some of the people who have heard them," Jonathan said.

Joe stood up and stretched. "Let's take a walk and forget about all these ghosts."

"Where do you want to go?" Mandie asked as the others rose, also.

"Why don't we go through the tunnel? I always find that a fascinating place," Jonathan suggested.

"All right. I'll get the key and we can go in from the outside door," Mandie said, starting toward the door.

Snowball, her white cat, pushed the door open and came in, purring very loudly as he rubbed around her ankles.

"He wants to go, too," Jonathan said, laughing. "There are probably lots of rats down there in that tunnel."

"Oh please, don't even mention such things," Celia said with a shiver.

"I'll be right back with the key," Mandie said, going out into the hall. Turning back she whispered, "Please don't talk about it too loudly, or someone else might want to go, too."

"Like a little Irish girl?" Jonathan asked with a grin.

Mandie nodded and continued into the hallway.

Mandie returned with the key, and the group managed to get out of the house without anyone knowing where they were going. They hurried down the hill to the outside entrance of the tunnel. When Mandie unlocked the door, she told the others, "There are lanterns and matches here."

Joe picked up a match and lit a lantern. He passed the glowing lantern to Mandie and said, "I think we'd better light more than one. Remember the time our lantern went out and we were in complete darkness way up the tunnel?"

"Of course I do. That wasn't any fun," Mandie said as Jonathan picked up another lantern and lit it. Then he held the lantern just inside the tunnel so they could all see. The walls were mainly dirt and rocks.

Snowball scooted into the tunnel between everyone's legs and quickly dashed ahead. Suddenly he stopped, and his fur stood straight up and he growled.

Everyone stopped to look. Joe flashed his lantern ahead. He laughed with relief and told the others, "It's a possum. How did he get in here?"

"How are we going to get him out?" Mandie wondered.

The possum sat there frozen, its eyes glittering in the light of the lantern while everyone looked at it.

"Well, we have to do something," Joe said, looking around. "Here, if everyone will step up on this ledge here, I'll see if I can chase him outside."

Everyone quickly stepped up to the ledge. Joe picked up a long stick and began waving it at the possum.

Mandie suddenly remembered something she learned once. "The light blinds him! And Snowball is probably scaring him. Come here, Snowball. Get out of the way!" she called to her cat.

Snowball didn't move and continued growling at the possum.

Suddenly John Shaw came up into the tunnel. "I was sent after y'all to come to dinner," he said. "What are you doing?" Just then he saw the possum and the cat. He reached down and quickly picked up Snowball, securely holding his paws so he couldn't scratch. "Now poke him with that stick, Joe. Give him a shove. He'll run."

Joe gave the possum a good poke, and the animal went running on out of the tunnel, with everyone following and laughing. They extinguished their lanterns and set them at the doorway.

As Mandie locked the door, her uncle said, "I wonder how that animal got inside the tunnel? I found the door unlocked the other day but figured I must have forgotten to lock it when I was in there a while ago."

"Uncle John, you never leave doors unlocked," Mandie said as they walked up the hill.

"I'm sure I do sometimes," John Shaw said. "Like if I'm interrupted or something. But I'll come back after we eat and make sure that possum is gone—and there aren't others."

Mandie handed him the key and said, "Now, don't forget I gave the key to you." She paused, then added, "You know, Uncle John, even if you did leave the door unlocked, it was closed, and the possum couldn't possibly have opened the door to get in."

John Shaw laughed and said, "No, the possum could not have opened the door. But the door was not closed all the way when I found it unlocked the other day. Several days ago I was out here working, but I had to leave quickly to meet someone at the house, and I'm sure I just didn't close the door all the way in my hurry." He smiled down at her and added, "No mystery about it, blue eyes."

Mandie grasped his hand as she said, "If you say so."

The day finally came when Mandie and Celia had to go back to school. Joe escorted them back to Charleston, and Jonathan and his father left in their special train car for New York. Uncle Ned, Morningstar, and Sallie went back to their home, but Mrs. Taft and Mrs. Hamilton stayed on awhile with Elizabeth and John Shaw.

Mr. Ryland met Mandie, Celia, and Joe at the depot with the carriage. Mary Lou was with him. She told them her mother would like for them all to come to their house for supper.

"Joe would like to see the college," Mandie told her as they boarded the carriage. "We have plenty of time for that, don't we?"

"Yes, we won't eat until six. Let's go on to the college first, then," Mary Lou decided.

Mr. Ryland waited with the carriage while Joe, Mandie, Celia, and Mary Lou walked around the college.

"The buildings are very impressive," Joe remarked as he looked around.

When they entered the front door of the main building, Mandie saw a lot of the girls sitting around the reception area. They all paused in their conversations to stare at Joe.

Mandie said under her breath to Celia, "I knew they would do that." They walked around the lobby and went into the sitting room, where more girls were talking. They, too, paused to look at Joe.

"You'd think these girls had never seen a man before," Mary Lou remarked under her breath.

"They haven't seen this one before, and they're just wondering who he is," Mandie whispered back.

"You have a beautiful college." Joe complimented the girls on their choice of school.

As they walked back up the driveway to return to the carriage, Mandie saw George Stuart and his friend arrive in another carriage. George looked at Mandie and Joe and said to his friend, "Now, *they* must have been properly introduced."

Mandie hurried to board the carriage with her friends.

"He always has to turn up," Mandie mumbled to Celia.

"Like he's watching for you," Celia whispered back.

Mr. and Mrs. Dunnigan made Joe welcome, and everyone enjoyed the visit. Then Mr. Dunnigan insisted that Joe spend the night with them instead of in that lonely hotel. Joe finally agreed, and they went to get his things from the depot.

Then Mandie insisted that Joe should come and see their

boardinghouse and meet Mrs. Thomason.

Mrs. Thomason was very friendly with Joe, and he smiled when he asked, "Now, what about that ghost you have living here?"

Mrs. Thomason laughed and said, "Oh, it's not really a ghost. It's some devilish boys."

Joe looked at Mandie and Celia and said, "You see, you don't really have a ghost living here."

"I didn't believe it anyway," Mandie told him.

Classes wouldn't be starting for another day, so Mandie, Celia, and Mary Lou saw Joe off on the train the next day.

"I'll see you at Christmastime," Joe called to Mandie and Celia as he waved from the open window of the train.

"Yes, see you then!" Mandie replied as the train pulled out of the station, huffing and puffing and ringing its bell.

The minute the noise was low enough that they could talk, Mary Lou said, "I've been wanting to tell you, but didn't want to say so in front of your friend Joe, but Grace Wilson went somewhere during the holidays after all. The day after y'all left she disappeared. Someone said she had been invited to someone's house for the holidays. I'm so glad for her."

"Oh yes, I am, too," Mandie agreed as they boarded their carriage. "But I wonder where she went. Whose house?"

"I'll probably hear about it in my music class tomorrow," Celia said.

And she did hear about it. Grace had stayed with the woman

who ran the sewing group that made clothes for poor children in the orphanage.

"And I was hoping she had friends to visit," Mandie said after Celia relayed the information she had learned.

"Those people are her friends, I believe," Celia replied. "And I'm sure she really enjoys doing such things for people who can't afford anything nice. I would also help out with the sewing, but I don't know how I would go about getting acquainted with them."

"I would, too," Mandie said. "We'll have to find a way to get information about this place."

The next day Mary Lou reported that, after mentioning the sewing to her mother, Mrs. Dunnigan knew immediately who the group was. There was an orphanage across town, and several local women had organized a sewing group to help make clothes for the children. And they would gladly take any volunteers.

Mandie, Celia, and Mary Lou planned to go down there the next weekend and investigate.

———

When Saturday came, Mandie, Mary Lou, and Celia had Mr. Ryland drive them to the orphanage. It was a very old stone building, long and two stories high. Mrs. Perry, who was in charge, was a tall, slender woman with gray hair and spectacles. She was very friendly and was happy that the girls wanted to help with sewing clothes for the children in the orphanage.

"But I'm sorry to tell you, it is not done here. It is at Mrs.

Wilkes's house across town. I can give you the address and you can call on her if you like," she told them. She wrote down the name and address and gave it to Mandie.

"Thank you, Mrs. Perry. We'll go there and see Mrs. Wilkes." The girls thanked her and waved good-bye before climbing back into the carriage.

Mr. Ryland knew all the streets in Charleston, so it was no problem for him to find the address. When he pulled the carriage to a stop in front of a huge brick house, Mandie, Celia, and Mary Lou all looked at one another.

"Are you sure this is the right address?" Mandie asked Mary Lou.

Mary Lou glanced at the paper the woman had given them and said, "Yes, this is the right address."

"I suppose we can go knock on the door," Mandie said doubtfully.

A uniformed maid opened the door just moments after the girls knocked.

"We are looking for Mrs. Wilkes, who is in charge of the sewing group for the orphanage." Mandie was hesitant in her request.

"Yes, misses, come right in," the maid replied, opening the door wide. "I'll get her. Just have seats over there." She motioned to an open archway, through which could be seen chairs and sofas.

Mandie, Celia, and Mary Lou sat down on a settee near the door and waited.

In a few minutes the maid came back to say, "Mrs. Wilkes will be right with you."

"Thank you," the girls chorused.

Mrs. Wilkes was a young woman, not much older than the girls. She seemed to be very stylish in the way she presented herself, and she was smiling and friendly.

"Welcome, young ladies," she said as she entered the room and took a seat across from them. "I am Mary Wilkes, and I understand you were inquiring about the sewing group we have for the orphanage."

"Yes, ma'am, we would like to help," Mandie replied. "I am Mandie Shaw, and these are my friends, Celia Hamilton and Mary Lou Dunnigan. We go to the Charleston Ladies' College, and we have some free time we could devote to your sewing project."

"We can always use more hands. It's so nice of you all to volunteer," Mrs. Wilkes said. "The orphanage doesn't have much money, and the little girls' clothes are shabby. I put together this sewing group for ladies who wanted to help. You see, the Charleston Cloth Company donates the material, and we make garments for the children to wear." She paused slightly, then added, "I assume you all do know how to sew."

"Yes, ma'am," the three chorused.

"I also know how to knit and embroider," Mandie added.

"So do I," Mary Lou said.

"That is wonderful," Mrs. Wilkes said. "I know that since you girls are in college, you won't have a whole lot of time to do such work, but anything at all that y'all can do would be most appreciated."

"How often do you meet?" Mandie asked.

"We have get-togethers once a month, but the volunteers are welcome here whenever they have time to sew."

By the time the girls left, they had agreed to come back to Mrs. Wilkes's house the next Saturday and spend the afternoon sewing with whomever else was there.

"I think I'm going to enjoy doing this sewing," Mandie said as they rode back to Mary Lou's house. "Especially since it is for orphans," she added.

"I am, too," Celia said.

"It will be something worthwhile to do with our time," Mary Lou said.

"Maybe we will see Grace Wilson here next Saturday. I wonder what she will think when she sees us," Mandie said. "I hope she doesn't think we are following her."

"I'm sure she will appreciate our wanting to help," Celia said.

Mandie thought about Grace and wondered if she was an orphan herself. Was that why she volunteered for the sewing group? Mandie promised herself that she would get acquainted with Grace Wilson.

chapter 9

The next Saturday Mandie, Celia, and Mary Lou returned to Mrs. Wilkes's house to participate in the sewing for the children. There were four other people helping: an older woman, a middle-aged woman, and two teenage girls, all of whom were friendly. The girls were daughters of the women and were still in school.

Mrs. Wilkes introduced them and said, "There seems to be a lot going on at the college today, so many girls won't be here."

Mandie, Celia, and Mary Lou looked at each other curiously.

"Oh, that's right." Celia suddenly remembered. "The chorus is practicing today, but I'm not in the chorus."

"I know that some of the art students are making posters for the music program, too," Mary Lou added.

"Maybe we can come back next Saturday, too, when there are more ladies here," Mandie said, looking at the stack of little dresses awaiting finishing touches. She picked up a dress with a scalloped collar and said, "I think I'll work on this one today."

Celia and Mary Lou also selected dresses to finish. Some needed buttonholes, some needed hemming, some needed the stitching to be finished. They each took a dress and went to sit at a long table.

Mandie looked at the dress she was working on and thought about how much prettier it would be if it were embroidered. Looking at one of the ladies, she asked, "Is there any embroidery thread that I could use?"

"Oh yes, dear, look on that table over by the window. It has lots of embroidery thread, buttons, and lace on it. Just take whatever you need," she told Mandie.

Mandie saw that the table held lots of different colors of thread, but she chose a pink color to embroider French knots on the collar of the little dress she was working on.

The three girls became so absorbed in their work that by the time they noticed the clock, they saw it was already suppertime. They all reluctantly laid down their work, said good-bye to Mrs. Wilkes, and headed toward the front door.

"It was wonderful having you young ladies here today," Mrs. Wilkes told them, walking them to the door. "I do hope you all will be able to return next Saturday."

"Unless something comes up to prevent it, we will be here," Mandie replied. "We enjoy doing this work."

The girls filed outside to find Mr. Ryland and his carriage; if they were out much longer, Mrs. Dunnigan would start to worry.

———————

The following Saturday when Mandie, Celia, and Mary Lou returned, Grace Wilson was already there, working on a small dress. Mandie immediately approached Grace.

"Hello, Grace, I'm Mandie Shaw. I'm glad to finally meet you," Mandie said, smiling at the girl.

Grace looked up from her work and gave Mandie a tight-lipped smile. "I'm glad to meet you, also." Then she continued working on the little dress.

Mandie glanced at her friends, then turned back to Grace and asked, "Do you mind if we sit here at the table with you?"

"Of course not," Grace answered, barely looking at Mandie. "There's plenty of room."

When Mandie tried to talk to her, Grace said, "I'm sorry, but what I'm doing here requires that I count stitches, and I'm not very good at counting stitches and carrying on a conversation."

"I'm sorry. I should pay more attention to my work, too," Mandie replied with a smile.

Grace left not long after they had arrived, and Mandie didn't get a chance to talk to her.

Mandie, Celia, and Mary Lou went to Mrs. Wilkes's to help with the sewing for the next two Saturdays, but they didn't see

Grace there anymore. She was always in her classes but was never seen around the school.

Then suddenly the Christmas holidays arrived. Everyone was excited about going home for the two weeks' break. Joe came to escort Mandie home, and Celia's aunt Rebecca came for Celia.

"Your mother is already at the Shaws' house, so we are going on the train with Mandie and Joe," Aunt Rebecca told Celia.

"But I thought we were going home first for our own gift-giving, and then going on to Mandie's house," Celia told her.

"Your mother changed plans, and she has all our gifts with her," Aunt Rebecca explained.

Mr. Jason Bond, Mandie's uncle's caretaker, met them at the depot in Franklin, North Carolina, when the train came in. Abraham was also there with the wagon to carry the luggage home.

"Welcome home, missy," Mr. Bond greeted Mandie.

"Is Grandmother here yet?" Mandie asked as she boarded the rig.

"Yes, miss, she got in last night," Mr. Bond replied. "You ladies get in the rig while I load the luggage into the wagon."

"I'll help you," Joe said, following Jason Bond toward the train to get the luggage.

They were ready to go a few minutes later, and when Joe climbed into the rig, Mandie said, "I wonder if Grandmother brought Senator Morton with her."

"I don't imagine so, not with Mr. Guyer being expected for the holidays," Joe replied.

"Is Jonathan coming with his father?" Celia asked.

"As far as I know he is," Joe said.

When they got to the house, everyone stepped into the parlor for a few minutes to speak to Elizabeth, Mandie's mother, and John Shaw. Dr. and Mrs. Woodard were there, also, as well as Celia's mother.

Elizabeth asked Celia's aunt Rebecca, "Did you not bring Mollie?"

"No, we left her with friends who have a daughter Mollie's age. The two girls are great friends, and we thought that since it is Christmastime and there are no children here at your house, it would be more enjoyable for her to stay with the Garrisons."

"That's probably better for her," Elizabeth agreed.

"Where is Grandmother, Mother?" Mandie asked.

"She's in her room resting right now, but I'm sure she'll be down shortly when she hears you have arrived," Elizabeth replied.

"Come on, Celia, let's go say hello to Aunt Lou. Then we can change into something more comfortable than these traveling suits," Mandie said.

In the kitchen Aunt Lou, the Shaws' housekeeper, was supervising Liza, the young maid, and Jennie, the cook. When Mandie and Celia entered the room, Aunt Lou hurried to embrace Mandie.

"So glad my chile has come home," she said as she squeezed Mandie's shoulders.

"And I'm glad to be home, Aunt Lou," Mandie said,

returning the embrace. "I miss all of you when I'm at school. I look forward to the day I'll be done with school and I'll be able to stay home."

Snowball, who perked up when Mandie and Celia walked into the kitchen, jumped out of the woodbox behind the big iron cookstove and was rubbing around Mandie's legs. Mandie stooped to pick him up.

"Oh, Snowball, I've missed you, too," she whispered to the cat as she stroked his fur.

Aunt Lou turned to Celia. "It's awfully nice seeing you, too. You need to come and visit a spell with my chile one of these days!" She gave Celia a quick hug.

"I hope I can when we get all caught up with everything at school," Celia replied.

Mandie sniffed the air and said, "I smell something awfully good cooking."

"That's the stew meat and potatoes on the stove over there," Aunt Lou explained.

"It smells so good," Mandie told Jennie. Then she turned to Liza, who was getting a pot out of the cupboard, and said, "I'm glad to see you, too, Liza. I hope you've been behaving lately." She grinned at the girl.

"I sho' has," Liza told her. Then moving closer, she whispered, "That Miss Sweet Thang, she come home and brung that April Snow with her. Ain't seen 'em, but her cook told me."

Mandie was surprised. "Polly Cornwallis brought April Snow

home with her?" The Cornwallises were the Shaws' next-door neighbors, and Polly was always a troublemaker.

"She sho' did," Liza said. "Them two must be up to sumpin'. They knows the boys are gonna be here."

"Well, I hope they don't come over," Mandie said with a frown.

"Oh, Mandie," Celia said, "Polly always comes over when she knows Joe is here."

"Liza, git the table set right now," Aunt Lou told the girl, shaking her big white apron at her.

"Yessum," Liza replied. She quickly left the kitchen through the door to the dining room.

"We'll see y'all later, when y'all are not quite so busy," Mandie said to Aunt Lou and Jennie. "Come on, Celia, let's go change our clothes."

Celia shared Mandie's room when she came to visit, and the girls talked and laughed as they quickly changed into fresh dresses and went back downstairs to the parlor.

All the talk centered around Christmas gifts. Jonathan and his father were expected the next day, and Uncle Ned, his wife, Morningstar, and their granddaughter, Sallie, would be arriving anytime.

"I hope we don't get a heavy snowstorm before Uncle Ned and his family arrive. They might have trouble crossing that mountain in his wagon," John Shaw said.

"I don't think a snowstorm would stop Uncle Ned from getting here," Dr. Woodard said. "The Cherokee people are capable of getting through any kind of weather."

Mandie and her friends quietly sat down at the far end of the huge parlor and listened to the adults' conversation.

"Well, I am certainly glad you have come to stay here until the holidays are over," John Shaw told Dr. Woodard.

"Yes, I thought it best to get here early and stay for the whole event," Dr. Woodard replied.

It was apparent they were discussing the expected baby of Elizabeth and John Shaw; however, a more-detailed conversation would not be appropriate in the presence of young unmarried people.

Mandie remembered the baby her mother had had shortly after she married John Shaw. The little boy didn't live. Mandie silently said a prayer that this baby would be born healthy and live to grow old. She glanced at her friends and knew they were also offering up prayers for her.

Mrs. Taft appeared in the doorway just then. "Well, I see the young ones have arrived," she said, walking over to Mandie.

Mandie stood up to embrace her, and Mrs. Taft said, "I know you and your friends will enjoy the peace and quiet of this house after what you've been through at the college."

"Oh yes, Grandmother," Mandie said. "And I'm so glad you are here. Is Senator Morton coming, too?"

Mrs. Taft looked at her and smiled. "Not this time, dear." She leaned closer to say, "You see, that New York friend of mine is due in at any time now."

"Mr. Guyer! Is Jonathan coming with him?" Mandie asked.

"Why, of course, dear. Jonathan wouldn't dare miss a few days here with you girls," Mrs. Taft said. "Now, I must go see what the grown-ups are talking about." She patted Mandie's shoulder, then went to sit with the adults.

Mandie turned back to Celia and Joe. "She said Jonathan is coming. I hope it is in time to go with us to cut the Christmas tree."

Joe glanced out the front window. "It's beginning to snow."

Mandie and Celia rose and walked over to the window to watch the white flakes tumbling down from the sky.

"Those large flakes mean the snow will remain on the ground awhile," Mandie said. "I wish Jonathan and Sallie would hurry up and get here."

Within the next hour Jonathan and his father arrived. Uncle Ned and his family arrived in their covered wagon shortly afterward.

When everyone was settled, John Shaw organized a group to go find a tree in the woods behind his house. After it was cut down, they put it in a stand and brought it into the wide front hallway. Everyone helped decorate it.

The young people surveyed the tree and Mandie said, "Now we might as well put our presents under it."

There was much secretive business of wrapping presents and stacking them under the tree. Mandie and her friends laughed as they tried to guess what everyone had wrapped.

"Since we are not allowed to pick them up and feel them, we might as well stop guessing," Mandie told her friends. "A wrapped present never is what I think it is, anyhow." She sighed and sat down on a bench to look at the tree in its colorful splendor.

The days passed quickly and Christmas Eve arrived, without any falling snow, and the entire household went to the midnight Christmas services at the church across the road.

Mandie and Celia talked for a long time when they got into bed that night. Finally, around two o'clock in the morning, Mandie suggested they go down to the kitchen and get some warm milk.

"If we are very quiet, we won't wake anyone," Mandie whispered to Celia as they silently descended the main staircase. A lamp was kept burning at the end of the hall next to the kitchen all night. Mandie picked the lamp up and took it with them into the kitchen.

"I hope there's plenty of milk," Mandie said, opening the wooden icebox.

At that moment, a baby's cry caused Mandie to freeze with her hand in the air, and she turned to Celia. "Did you hear that?" she asked in a whisper.

"Yes," Celia whispered back.

"Do you think the baby is here already?" Mandie asked excitedly, taking out the pitcher of milk and closing the door.

"Maybe," Celia said.

Suddenly there was a louder cry. Mandie quickly set the pitcher on the table and reached to embrace Celia. "The baby must be here!"

"Yes, I think so!" Celia was nearly as excited as Mandie.

The two stood there for a few moments and listened for more cries, but there was not another sound.

Then suddenly the door opened and Aunt Lou hurried into the kitchen. She barely glanced at the girls and said, "Outta my way, chillen, gotta have hot water for them babies." She stoked up the fire in the big iron cookstove and got a pail to get hot water out of the heater attached to it.

"Aunt Lou, did you say *babies?* More than one?" Mandie was shaking with excitement.

"That's right. A boy and a girl," the older woman said, quickly carrying the bucket of hot water out of the room.

Mandie stood there frozen in excitement as she thought about her mother having not one but two babies. She hugged Celia and said, "Let's thank the Lord."

The two girls bowed their heads and gave thanks for the newcomers.

Finally pouring the milk into a small pot, Mandie set it on the firebox that was kept going in the iron cookstove all the time, and waited for it to warm a little.

Then, carefully pouring it into two cups, she told Celia, "I can't go back to bed. Let's go sit in the parlor."

The fire in the parlor fireplace had been banked for the night, but Mandie got the poker and stirred the hot coals until it began to flame up. They sat on two footstools in front of it.

To their surprise, Mrs. Taft came into the parlor, fully dressed, and sat down near them. "Thank the Lord, everything is fine this time," she said with a loud sigh of relief. "Amanda, you now have a little brother and a little sister."

Mandie was speechless as she stared at her grandmother with her mouth open.

"Your mother is resting peacefully now," Mrs. Taft added.

"Oh, Grandmother, I've been so worried about her, after losing my little brother the first time," Mandie said, moving over to put her head in her grandmother's lap as tears covered her face.

"Now, now, child, there's nothing to cry about. It's a time to rejoice," Mrs. Taft said, running her fingers through Mandie's long blond hair. "I see you girls have milk. I wonder if you would go with me to help me fix a cup." She stood up.

"Of course, Grandmother," Mandie said, rising. "But why don't you just sit back down and I'll go get some for you. It won't take but a minute or two." She left her cup on the table and headed for the kitchen.

After Mandie returned with another cup of milk, Mrs. Taft and the two girls sat by the fire the rest of the night. Gradually everyone else joined them, and by sunup everyone had assembled in the parlor, except her uncle and her mother.

Finally, when her uncle appeard in the doorway, he was wearing a big grin and said to Mandie, "Come with me, little blue eyes. I have a wonderful Christmas present for you."

"I know," Mandie said with a quick laugh as she rose and joined him.

John Shaw took her to her mother's room to see the babies

who lay in a bassinet, quietly sleeping. Mandie bent to inspect them. They looked identical. "Oh, Uncle John, aren't they wonderful!"

Mandie's mother spoke from the huge canopied bed. "Amanda, you must name them. Your uncle and I decided we want you to do that for us."

Mandie quickly went to stand by the bed and hold her mother's hand. "But, Mother, I named my little brother, remember? Maybe you and Uncle John should name these two."

Elizabeth squeezed her hand and said, "No, dear, we can't agree on names, so we decided to leave it up to you."

Mandie turned to glance at the two babies and said, "Well, now, let me see." She hummed under her breath a few seconds and then said, "Since it is Christmas, the girl should be Carol, like a Christmas carol, but what is there for a boy that would go with that?" She frowned as she thought about it.

"Why not a name beginning with a C for him?" Elizabeth suggested.

"Let's see, Clyde, Charles, Christopher. No, I don't like any of those," Mandie decided. "How about Carl?" She quickly looked at her uncle.

"That's just perfect." John Shaw smiled as he reached to embrace Mandie.

"Yes, those are good names for twins: Carol and Carl," Elizabeth said.

Mandie squeezed her mother's hand as she said, "This is the most wonderful Christmas present I have ever had." She stooped to kiss her mother's cheek, then turned to give her uncle John a kiss on his cheek. "Thank you."

The holidays flew by and Mandie hated having to go back to college and leave her little brother and sister.

"At least I was home when they arrived," Mandie told her mother as she and Celia waited for Mr. Bond to take them and Celia's aunt Rebecca to the depot.

Joe was staying a few days longer to visit with his parents, and Celia's mother was glad that Rebecca had volunteered to escort the girls back to college.

More excitement would be waiting for them at the college.

chapter 10

When Mandie, Celia, and Aunt Rebecca arrived in Charleston, they found that Mr. Ryland and Mary Lou had been waiting for them. They all said good-bye to Celia's aunt Rebecca, who got on another train headed for her home.

"Y'all will never guess what happened while you were gone." Mary Lou was nearly bursting with her news.

"What?" Mandie and Celia asked simultaneously.

"There was a strange man in your boardinghouse," Mary Lou told them with nervous excitement.

"At *our* boardinghouse?" Mandie asked.

"Who saw him?" Celia asked.

As Mr. Ryland drove the carriage out of the depot parking lot, Mary Lou said, "You know Sadie, the girl who works in the kitchen? She was cleaning up after suppertime on Christmas Eve, and she saw the shadow of a man standing in the dining room, but then he suddenly disappeared."

"What did Sadie do?" Mandie asked wide-eyed.

"Sadie quit on the spot, but Mrs. Thomason was able to talk her into coming back when she promised Sadie that she would not be left alone anymore. Now what do you think about that?" Mary Lou drew a deep breath.

Mandie frowned and said, "Sadie is flighty sometimes, and she might have imagined it."

"Well, everyone believes her," Mary Lou replied.

Celia warily asked, "We are not going to stay in that boardinghouse any longer, are we, Mandie? Not with a strange man lurking about?"

"Of course. Where else can we stay?"

"Both of you can stay at my house," Mary Lou offered. "My mother has already told me to tell y'all that."

"Please, Mandie," Celia begged, near tears.

"Well, maybe just for tonight," Mandie said. "Until we have a chance to get to the bottom of this."

"I don't think I'm going to stay there at all anymore, as long as Mary Lou's mother will allow us to stay at her house," Celia said firmly.

"Maybe we ought to move back into the dormitory," Mandie suggested.

"No, that would be admitting defeat," Celia quickly responded. "Oh, I am beginning to hate this college."

Mandie looked at Celia and said, "Well, it's half term now. We could probably transfer to another college if you would like to."

"No, I like my music classes here. We'll just have to stay and muddle through the rest of the year somehow," Celia said.

"I'm sure my mother would be glad to have both of you stay with us this school year," Mary Lou said.

Mandie grinned at Mary Lou and said, "We'll just have to solve this mystery by the time our sophomore year begins."

"I'll help with anything I can," Mary Lou offered.

Mr. Ryland pulled the carriage to a stop in front of the boardinghouse just then. Mandie leaned forward and said, "I'm sorry, but it appears we'll be going to the Dunnigans' house, Mr. Ryland."

He nodded and said, "As you wish, miss," and drove on.

Mrs. Dunnigan was on the front porch waiting for them.

"I wanted to be sure you all came on here," she told Mandie and Celia. "You are very welcome. Come on inside. I prepared a room for y'all. I was sure y'all wouldn't want to be going back to that boardinghouse right now."

"Thank you, Mrs. Dunnigan," Celia quickly said.

"We appreciate your hospitality," Mandie told her.

Mr. Dunnigan came out the front door, greeted the girls, and helped Mr. Ryland bring their trunks up to their bedroom.

"I know you young ladies are tired after that train trip, so go ahead and get comfortable while I see to dinner," Mrs. Dunnigan told Mandie and Celia as everyone stood at the door of the room. "The bathroom is down the hall there," she added, pointing. "When you are ready, just come on down to the parlor." She went back down the hallway toward the stairs.

"I'll wait for y'all down in the parlor," Mary Lou told them.

"Oh no, Mary Lou. Stay here and talk. We won't be long changing," Mandie said.

"Here, I'll hang up some of your dresses while y'all get dressed," Mary Lou offered as the girls opened their trunks.

"I'll change into *anything* to get out of this travel suit," Mandie said, pulling a dress out of her trunk.

"Me too," Celia added.

"You use the bathroom first to clean up while I help hang our clothes," Mandie said as she began taking clothes out of their trunks.

"I won't be long," Celia promised as she took clothes and hurried down the hallway.

"I would like to walk around to the boardinghouse and talk to Mrs. Thomason after we eat," Mandie told Mary Lou.

Mary Lou smiled and said, "I knew you would want to do that. I would like to go with you."

"I was hoping you would want to go," Mandie said as she pulled a blue dress trimmed with lace out of the trunk and hung it in the huge wardrobe. "I'd just like to hear what Mrs. Thomason has to say about strange men standing in her boardinghouse."

"Yes, something seems to have scared Sadie witless, and I'd like to know what it was."

"We'll have to find her and ask her about it, too," Mandie said. "You know, I feel so sorry for Celia because she is really upset."

"Maybe talking with Mrs. Thomason will help," Mary Lou said.

"Unless Mrs. Thomason really believes Sadie saw someone," Mandie replied.

Celia returned from the bathroom all clean and dressed. Mandie grabbed a dress and hurried into the bathroom to quickly wash and change for dinner.

Later, as they all sat at the supper table, Mandie tried to talk about anything other than Sadie's story because of Celia, but Celia kept bringing up the subject herself.

"Mrs. Dunnigan, did Mrs. Thomason say anyone else saw whatever Sadie claimed to see?" Celia asked.

"No, dear. Sadie was the only one," Mrs. Dunnigan replied. "But as I'm sure you know, Sadie is afraid of her own shadow, so her story may not be entirely correct. You will want to talk to Mrs. Thomason about it to be sure."

Mandie spoke up. "I thought we would go around there and speak to her after we finish eating." She paused to take another bite of her food, then added, "I don't suppose those fellows we see around our college now and then could be playing a joke, could they? They are always mentioning a ghost in the boardinghouse."

"But it happened while everyone was gone for the holidays, so I don't believe it could have been them," Mrs. Dunnigan said.

"But, Mother, the one who is always trying to talk to Mandie—George Stuart—is from England. Surely he wouldn't have gone all the way home for the holidays," Mary Lou reminded her.

"You're right, that's not likely," Mrs. Dunnigan said.

Then Mr. Dunnigan volunteered his own information. "Well,

I haven't seen any of those young fellows that you are talking about at all during the holidays, so evidently they went somewhere."

Mandie tried to hurry through the meal so she could get to the boardinghouse, but everyone else seemed to be awfully slow, including Celia, who she noticed didn't have much to say and had a worried look on her face. But finally the meal came to an end.

Mr. and Mrs. Dunnigan walked with the girls over to the boardinghouse. Mrs. Thomason herself opened the door and greeted them with a big smile.

"I'm so glad you young ladies are back. Come on in." She led the way into the parlor. No one else seemed to be about.

As soon as everyone was seated, Celia quickly got to the point. "Mrs. Thomason, did Sadie really see a strange man in your boardinghouse?"

Everyone was silent while Mrs. Thomason took a minute to reply. "You know, girls, we talked about the so-called ghost in this house when y'all first moved in, and we all agreed it was a silly prank by some of the boys when no one lived in the house." She paused. "Therefore, I believe it was just some boys trying to scare Sadie."

"But the house is lived in now, and the boarders were gone for the holidays, weren't they?" Celia asked.

"The house was not empty over the holidays, although most of my boarders did go home," Mrs. Thomason replied, and then straightening up to look at the girls, she added, "I believe Sadie imagined she saw someone. She is not the most level-headed person, and y'all know that firsthand."

"So you think Sadie just imagined the whole thing?" Mandie asked.

"Yes, I do," Mrs. Thomason replied. "You see, she had heard the boys' ghost stories so many times that evidently she believed them."

Mandie suddenly remembered the noise she and Celia had heard in their bedroom that night. "There was certainly something making a noise in or around our room when Celia and I first moved in. And we never did figure out what it was," she said quickly.

"Yes, that's right," Celia immediately added. "It was a strange scratching noise. We left the lamps on for the rest of the night."

"But we believed that noise could have been made by all those people checking in here that night," Mandie explained.

"Well, dear, you never told me about this. I might have had an explanation at that time, but now I don't know," Mrs. Thomason said.

"It never happened again," Mandie reassured Mrs. Thomason.

"Please be sure to let me know if it does, or if anything else strange, shall we say, happens," Mrs. Thomason told the girls.

"But, Mrs. Thomason, we are staying with the Dunnigans now," Celia told her.

Mrs. Dunnigan immediately spoke up. "I knew the girls would be upset when they heard of this incident, and I asked them to stay with us, at least until things settle down and get back to normal. I hope you don't mind."

"No, of course I don't mind. I know the girls will probably sleep better in your house for a few nights," Mrs. Thomason said, smiling at Celia and Mandie. "Some of the others are staying elsewhere for now and will be coming back to their rooms after the news dies down. In the meantime, if you girls would like to get anything you need from your room, I'd be glad to go up with you and help."

"No, ma'am. I took so much home for the holidays that I don't really need anything else right now," Mandie told her.

"Neither do I," Celia said.

Mandie suddenly remembered her good news. "I almost forgot to tell everyone the wonderful news! My mother had twins while we were home for Christmas. She named them Carol and Carl."

"How wonderful," Mrs. Thomason said. "I must figure out what kind of gift to send her."

"And I must write to her and offer my congratulations," Mrs. Dunnigan said.

"It's nice that you have a boy in the family now, and it's not all girls," Mr. Dunnigan added with a wink.

Mandie smiled and said, "Yes, sir, and I'm anxious to get back home and see them again."

"Spring holidays will certainly be welcome this year, won't they?" Mrs. Dunnigan said.

"Yes, ma'am," Mandie said, grinning. "And while we are talking about the holidays, I was going to ask Mary Lou if she could go home with me for the break in the spring, but since

we're talking about them now, maybe you would let me know now
if she can."

"But, Mandie, you haven't even asked me if I want to go,"
Mary Lou said teasingly.

"Since I am always visiting your house, I figured you might like
to go home with me for a change," Mandie said, grinning at her.

"Of course, Mary Lou has permission to go visit at your
house, if that is satisfactory with your mother, Amanda," Mrs.
Dunnigan said.

Mandie looked at Mary Lou and said, "Then you will be
spending the spring holidays at my house, and I imagine that Celia
will, too?" She looked questioningly at Celia.

"Of course, I always spend the holidays at your house,
Mandie," Celia said with a sigh, then added, "But I am expecting
everyone to come to my house for at least part of the summer
vacation."

"I'd like to come to your house for a while this summer, Celia,"
Mandie told her. "However, you understand that I have to spend
some time with my new little sister and brother."

"Since I've always lived in the city, I would enjoy visiting your
farm, Celia, and seeing all the horses," Mary Lou said.

Celia looked at Mandie and said, "Well then, as soon as we
can arrange the times with our other friends, we can make plans
for the summer holidays."

Later, after leaving the boardinghouse, the conversation
continued between the girls' bedrooms through the connecting
door until way into the morning.

When the early morning sunshine woke Mandie, she stretched and poked Celia to wake her.

"We have the whole day off today. What are we going to do?" Mandie asked as Celia sat up and looked around the room.

Celia yawned and replied, "Let's just be lazy and do nothing."

"Maybe Mary Lou has some plans," Mandie said as she sat up and propped against her pillow.

Mary Lou came to the doorway in her nightgown and asked, "Did I hear my name?"

"Yes, what are your plans for today?" Mandie asked, flipping around to sit on the side of the bed.

"I don't really have any, but since today is Saturday, we could check on the sewing group and see if they are working on the children's clothes today," Mary Lou replied. "That is, if y'all want something to do."

"Oh yes, let's do that," Celia said, sliding to the edge of the bed and stretching.

"Well, we can have Mr. Ryland bring us to the sewing group this morning," Mandie suggested. "Maybe we'll see Grace Wilson working there today."

By the time everyone had finished the hearty breakfast Mrs. Dunnigan put on the table, Mr. Ryland had the carriage parked in front of the house and was waiting for them.

When they arrived at Mrs. Wilkes's house, quite a large assortment of people had already assembled and were busy sewing.

Mandie quickly looked around the large room as she and her friends walked over to the table to select something to work on. She didn't see Grace. As she and Celia and Mary Lou stood at the table, she mentioned it to them, then said, "In fact, I don't see anyone I recognize."

"Neither do I," Celia said.

"Let's do some work for a while and maybe someone we know will come later," Mary Lou suggested.

Although they worked for several hours, no one else came.

When Mr. Ryland came back to get them, Mary Lou said, "Why don't we drive by the college? We won't be able to stop, though, because my mother will be waiting for us to come home and eat."

"All right. We might happen to see someone we know," Mandie agreed.

When they got to the college, Mr. Ryland brought the carriage to a halt in the parking space and asked, "Will you be going inside, misses?"

"No, Mr. Ryland, we won't have time to do that. We were just thinking we might see someone we know," Mandie replied.

"Look, isn't that George Stuart in the carriage parked down the driveway?" Celia asked.

Mandie glanced at the carriage, then quickly looked away. "Yes, it is. I'd really like to find out if he was here during the holidays, but I don't dare walk up to him and ask him," she said. Then, smiling, she added, "Remember, we haven't been properly introduced."

"His friend is with him, too—the one we always see," Celia said.

"And I do believe that is his sister coming out of the dormitory. She's walking toward his carriage," Mary Lou said.

At that moment George Stuart, his friend, and his sister all looked their way.

The girls quickly turned their attention to others moving about the campus.

"Why don't we go, Mandie? I feel strange just sitting here and looking at everybody," Celia said.

"You're right. We need to get back to Mary Lou's house, anyway," Mandie agreed as she leaned forward and spoke to Mr. Ryland. "We'll go back to the Dunnigans' now, please, Mr. Ryland."

"Yes, miss," the driver replied.

When they arrived at the Dunnigans' house, they found Mrs. Dunnigan in the parlor. "Mrs. Thomason has been doing a little investigative work," she told them. "You all may be interested to know that George Stuart and his friends from England, including his sister, did not leave Charleston during the holidays, but were seen all around town."

"Then they could have played a trick on Sadie," Mandie said as she sat on the settee.

"How could they do that with Mrs. Thomason in the house? She always keeps the doors locked, day and night," Celia reminded her.

"Maybe they saw Sadie outside somewhere and teased her about a ghost," Mary Lou suggested.

Mandie had a sudden idea. "What if they have a key?" she

asked excitedly, looking at everyone.

"That may be possible, but how did they get it?" Mrs. Dunnigan asked. "I'm sure she wouldn't have left the key around for someone to steal."

"But the school would have had a key. And remember all those tales about people being seen in the house when it was empty?" Mandie reminded them. "Anyone could have made a duplicate."

"Yes, it looks like it is very possible that someone could have broken into the house," Mrs. Dunnigan said. "I wonder if Mrs. Thomason has thought about changing the locks."

Mary Lou frowned and said, "Didn't everyone say that when the house was empty, someone kept breaking a window to get into the house?"

"We need to discuss this further with Mrs. Thomason," Mrs. Dunnigan said. "In the meantime, our meal is ready, if you young ladies would like to freshen up."

The three girls went to the bathroom on the first floor to wash up and comb their hair and discuss the suggestions that had been made.

Mandie decided they had to get to the bottom of this mystery.

chapter 11

Mandie and her friends did not get a chance to talk with Mrs. Thomason over the weekend because she was busy with new tenants checking into her boardinghouse.

Monday morning the girls had to return to classes at the college. As Mr. Ryland brought their carriage to a stop in front of the school, Mandie saw George Stuart and his friend driving away.

"I do declare, I believe that fellow hangs around here an awful lot," Mandie commented.

"He evidently drives his sister around, so he would be coming here a lot," Mary Lou said.

As the three stepped down from the carriage, Celia added, "His sister must need to be where we always are."

Even though the three were early entering the chapel, several other girls were already there. As Mandie, Celia, and Mary Lou sat down near the front, Mandie noticed George Stuart's sister and another girl sitting across the aisle. The two girls saw Mandie sit down, then immediately bent their heads close together and began talking behind their hands, looking up now and then to smile and giggle.

"I suppose we must be the topic of their conversation," Mandie said under her breath to Celia and Mary Lou as they tried to avoid eye contact with the giggling girls.

"They are acting very unladylike right here in chapel. I wonder if anyone will notice and take points off for their deportment," Celia said.

"That's a very good question. We just need to ignore such behavior," Mary Lou said.

"That's right. Let's just pretend they don't exist right now," Mandie said. "I'm more interested in getting an opportunity to ask Mrs. Thomason about the keys to her house."

At that moment Mandie saw Polly Cornwallis and April Snow come into the room together, go directly to George Stuart's sister, and sit down near her. The girl stopped talking to her friend to say something to Polly. April and Polly turned slightly to look at Mandie, then turned away when they saw they were seen.

"So the two troublemakers are friends of George Stuart's sister," Mandie said to Mary Lou and Celia. "That might explain a lot of things."

"Yes," Celia agreed.

"I remember you said those two like to stir up trouble," Mary Lou whispered.

"And they know how to do it," Mandie said.

There was a soft tap on the pulpit at the front of the room.

Reverend Coggins cleared his throat and greeted the audience. "Good morning, young ladies."

About half of the audience replied, "Good morning."

Mandie's mind wandered over the problem at the boardinghouse, and before she realized it, Reverend Coggins was dismissing them. She had not heard a word he had said. She was ashamed of herself and resolved to pay close attention next time.

As soon as classes were over for the day, the three girls hurried to the carriage. They would have to eat at the Dunnigans' first and then go see Mrs. Thomason.

Luckily the meal was over in a hurry, because Mr. Dunnigan had to return to his office to finish some work. Mrs. Dunnigan had visitors coming for afternoon tea, and she declined the invitation to go with the girls to the boardinghouse.

"Supper will be promptly at six o'clock," Mrs. Dunnigan reminded the girls.

"Yes, ma'am," they replied in unison.

The girls walked around the block to the boardinghouse, and Mandie used her key to let them in. They found Mrs. Thomason in the office with Miss Flora doing paper work.

As the girls stood at the doorway of the office, Mandie said, "We apologize for interrupting. We'll just sit out here in the hall until you are free. We wanted to ask you some questions, Mrs. Thomason, if you don't mind."

"I should be free in about fifteen minutes," she told the girls. "There is fresh coffee out there on the buffet. Help yourselves, and I'll join you shortly.

The girls took cups of coffee and sat in the parlor. It wasn't long until Mrs. Thomason entered the room with her own cup of coffee and sat down.

Mandie was so eager to ask questions that she spoke immediately. "Mrs. Thomason, we've been wondering if you had the locks on the house changed when you rented it from the college."

"Why yes, dear, I did. That was my first priority when I leased the house," Mrs. Thomason replied. "I had no idea as to how many people had keys at that time."

"So if someone used a key to get in here, it would have to be a key you had given them," Mandie figured.

"Why yes, and I only gave keys to people who were living here," Mrs. Thomason explained. "I wanted to be sure that I knew exactly who had keys to my house."

"On the other hand, if someone had lived here and moved out, even though they would have returned the keys to you, they could have had a duplicate made, couldn't they?" Mary Lou asked.

"Well, yes, I suppose so, but why would anyone want to keep a key they no longer had any use for?" Mrs. Thomason asked, puzzled with this question, and then she dismissed it. "Well, I've only been here a short while, and there haven't been that many people who have lived here while I've run this place, so I haven't given out many keys."

"But you have had people rent rooms for just a short time, haven't you?" Celia asked.

"I try to rent to long-term boarders, so we don't have a

turnover too often, but there have been a few who stayed only a few nights," Mrs. Thomason replied. "I see what you girls are thinking. You believe someone must have a key and came back to scare Sadie. Is that right?" She looked at the three girls.

"I think someone has a key that you don't know about. How else would they be able to get into the house?" Mandie asked. "And I don't think anyone living here would dare play tricks like that."

"No, I would hope not," Mrs. Thomason said thoughtfully. "Your reasoning could be the solution to this mystery. I suppose I should try to track down anyone who has ever lived here. But I am sure every ex-tenant has returned the keys when they left. That is our first request when anyone checks out."

"But if they had a duplicate key made, they could still get in," Mandie said. "And I suppose there's no way to check that out."

"We could go see all the key makers and ask if anyone who lived here had keys made," Celia suggested.

"But there must be lots of key makers here in this town," Mary Lou said. "I don't know where any are located, but in a town the size of Charleston, there must be quite a few."

"No," Mrs. Thomason stated as she shook her head. "When I leased the house, I had to look for one to change the locks, and I found only one anywhere near here who could do the old-fashioned locks and give me new keys."

"Then they would have a record of your new locks and would know whether any more keys have been made, wouldn't they?" Mandie asked excitedly.

"If they keep records. They are a very small place, and I paid them cash. I know they didn't give me a receipt," Mrs. Thomason explained.

"We could at least talk to them, though, couldn't we?" Mandie asked.

"Yes, I suppose so, but I would have to go with you. They wouldn't know you, and I doubt they would give any such information to a stranger," Mrs. Thomason explained.

"Would you be able to go with us to see these people tomorrow afternoon?" Mandie asked.

"I suppose I could arrange to leave the house that long. I don't go out very often these days because of Sadie. I'm afraid she might just leave again if I don't keep watch on her," Mrs. Thomason replied.

"I'll ask Mr. Ryland to come back after our noon meal tomorrow, and then we'll come around and get you," Mandie promised.

"Fine," Mrs. Thomason said, rising from her chair. "Now, I do have some office work that needs to get done."

"Yes, ma'am," all the girls said, also rising.

When Mandie and her friends got back to the Dunnigans', Mary Lou took them in through a side door.

"So we don't have to go through the parlor where all those ladies are," Mary Lou explained.

Mandie could hear a slight murmur of talking and low laughter as the girls passed through the hallway and went to the back room where the piano was kept.

As they sat down Mary Lou said, "I'm sure we can get some of the tea and sweetcakes my mother is serving if we slip back to the kitchen. Would y'all like some?"

"Yes," Celia quickly responded. "I'm absolutely tired out from all this excitement." She laughed.

"Come on. Let's see what we can round up." Mary Lou led the way back to the kitchen.

The girls drank tea and ate sweetcakes while chatting about their visit with Mrs. Thomason and what they believed the next day held in store for them.

———

After the noon meal the next day, Mr. Ryland drove the girls and Mrs. Thomason to the street address Mrs. Thomason had provided.

As he pulled the horse to a stop, Mrs. Thomason looked around and said, "This is a flower shop. We're looking for a locksmith, Mr. Ryland." She glanced at the address she had brought with her.

"But, madam, that locksmith closed up sometime before Christmas. This flower shop was here all during the Christmas holidays," Mr. Ryland told her.

Mrs. Thomason showed him the piece of paper and said, "Do you have any idea as to where this locksmith, Sol Jacks, might have moved?"

"As far as I can remember, I believe there was a sign in the window stating he was going out of business, and a notice was left for people to pick up any orders they had with him at that time," the driver replied.

"Oh dear, we are in a quandary now," Mrs. Thomason said with a loud sigh.

"Would it be possible to find where he lives?" Mandie asked.

"I believe he lived in the apartment above this shop," Mr. Ryland said. "I could ask among other drivers if they have any information concerning this man, if you please."

"Oh yes, please do. That would be most helpful," Mrs. Thomason said. "Perhaps another driver knew him."

"I will check and let you know, madam," Mr. Ryland promised.

Mrs. Thomason had to hurry back to her work at the boardinghouse, and after Mr. Ryland dropped her off, he brought the girls to the Dunnigans' house.

At the supper table that night the girls told Mr. and Mrs. Dunnigan about their attempted visit to the locksmith.

"Mr. Ryland promised to try to locate him for us," Mandie said.

"I believe that will be impossible," Mr. Dunnigan said, clearing his throat as he drank his coffee. "I had Sol Jacks put new locks on my office right before Christmas, and he told me he was retiring and going to sail the seas awhile before settling down again. There's no telling where the man is now."

"Oh no!" Mandie said.

"I don't know if there will be any way to find him," Mr. Dunnigan said. "He said he was leaving on a ship as a crew member for parts unknown, as he put it."

"Do you suppose he took everything with him? Maybe he just

left the paper work in the shop when he closed his business, since he wouldn't be needing it any longer," Celia said.

"That is a good point," Mandie said firmly.

"But if he left any papers, what would the flower shop have done with them when they moved in?" Mary Lou wondered aloud.

"You could always go back and ask the owner of the flower shop about this," Mrs. Dunnigan said.

"Let's do," Mandie agreed. "How about tomorrow afternoon?"

"Tomorrow afternoon would be fine," Celia replied as Mary Lou nodded her head.

The next day turned out to be a cloudy, chilly day, but the girls decided to go to the flower shop anyhow after their noon meal with the Dunnigans. Mr. Ryland put the top up on the carriage, and the three were too excited to feel the weather anyhow.

Mr. Ryland parked the carriage in an empty space directly in front of the flower shop.

As the girls stepped down from the vehicle, Mandie stopped in front of the shop window and said in surprise, "Look, Grace is inside."

"You're right." Mary Lou sounded confused.

"It looks like she's moving some flowerpots around," Celia said.

As the three hurried toward the door, Mandie paused to say, "Do you suppose Grace is working here?"

Mary Lou and Celia looked at her, and then the three looked at Grace through the window again.

"Well, she's definitely not acting like a customer," Celia said.

"Hm. Grace must be working here," Mandie decided as she pushed the door open.

"Hello, Grace," Mandie said, as the girl came to the front of the shop.

"Welcome!" Grace seemed surprised to see the girls there. "Are you interested in buying some flowers?"

"You work here?" Mary Lou asked.

"Yes, I work here after classes every day," Grace replied, going to move some more flowerpots.

"Do you enjoy working here?" Mandie asked, trying to think of something to say.

"Oh yes, the owner is a wonderful lady and gives me full authority when I am here alone, which is most of the time. You see, Mrs. Poinsett is elderly and unable to do everything required to own this shop," Grace explained.

"So this is why we don't see you at the sewing group anymore," Mandie said.

Grace shook her head. "I don't have time to go to Mrs. Wilkes's anymore, but I take little garments home with me and in my spare time I work on them then. I try to help whenever I can."

"It's so great that you have such worthwhile things to do while most of the other girls at school just loaf during their free time," Celia said.

The girls nodded their agreement. Then Mandie cleared her throat and asked, "Grace, do you know anything about the man who had the key shop here before it became this flower shop?"

Grace looked puzzled. "I don't know anything about the man. When Mrs. Poinsett opened this shop, I helped her clean out the mess he had left—papers everywhere, and it seemed like he hadn't cleaned in a year—but I never saw him. He left before I met Mrs. Poinsett."

"What papers?" Mandie asked. "Did they look like records? And what did y'all do with all the papers?"

Grace frowned as she replied, "The papers seemed to be a mix of orders and scrap paper. There were a lot of numbers and drawings. But we were in a hurry to get this place cleaned out, so we didn't look too closely. Oh, and there were a lot of old keys stuck here and there."

Mandie glanced at her friends, then asked hopefully, "What did y'all do with all that mess?" She held her breath, hoping Grace would say they had saved it.

"I'm not sure about all of it, but Mrs. Poinsett thought we should box up the papers in case the man came back for them someday."

"You saved all the papers?" Mary Lou asked excitedly. "Are they stored here in the shop?"

Grace looked curiously at the girls and said, "In the attic and in the basement. I must say, you girls certainly are interested in this man. Did y'all know him or something?"

The three looked at each other and then Mandie said, "This is very confidential information, Grace, and we ask that you not repeat it to anyone, but we need to see Mr. Jacks's records because we believe someone might have had a duplicate key made to Mrs. Thomason's boardinghouse. We need to find out exactly who had that duplicate made." She paused. "You see, we think someone used it to go inside and frighten a girl who works there."

"Oh yes, I heard about that so-called ghost appearing in the boardinghouse, but of course I thought it was just some story someone was making up," Grace said. "Do you mean to tell me that someone got inside the boardinghouse without permission and scared people? Why would anyone do that?"

"We don't really have any facts, but that's what we think," Mandie replied. "And we've discussed all this with Mrs. Thomason. I told her I believe someone copied a key and used it without her permission to get inside, maybe an ex-boarder, and she said she had all her keys made here when this was a key shop. So we are trying to track down a record of anyone who lived there, moved out and turned in their key, but had a copy of the key made so they could use it to get inside."

"Oh my!" Grace exclaimed. "Whoever would do such a thing? I can't imagine anyone bothering to sneak back inside to scare people. You know, they say there have always been rumors about that house being haunted."

"Yes, we know all about it," Mary Lou said. "I live around the corner from the boardinghouse, so we have always heard tales about a ghost, but we believed it was some devilish boys playing pranks."

"And the school boys seem to be the ones who are always telling the tales," Celia added.

"Do you think Mrs. Poinsett would give us permission to look

through all those old papers that belonged to the locksmith?"
Mandie asked.

"I think so, but I'd have to ask her to be sure before I could
allow anyone to do that," Grace replied. "Should I tell her the
reason for your desire to see the papers?"

Mandie looked at her two friends and Celia and Mary Lou
nodded. She turned back to Grace and nodded. "If you would
please ask her to keep all this very confidential. If word got out
about what we're doing, I'm sure someone would find a way to
stop us."

"All right then," Grace said. "I'll talk to Mrs. Poinsett tonight
when she comes to lock up, and if y'all will drop by tomorrow I'll
tell you what she has to say."

"Thank you, Grace," Mandie said. "Are you still living in the
dormitory? We never see you except now and then in different
classes."

"Oh yes, I'm still living in the dormitory. My scholarship
covers that," Grace replied

"You know, I am on a scholarship myself," Mary Lou told
Grace. "It doesn't cover living in the dormitory, but I don't need
it, since my parents live here in Charleston."

Grace smiled. "I am so grateful for mine. I couldn't have come
here without it. I'm looking forward to someday thanking the
person who set it up." She glanced at Mandie and, with a hint of
sadness in her voice, added, "I grew up the hard way and have to
work for my education."

Mandie frowned and wondered what she meant. Why would Grace say such a thing? As the girls turned to leave the shop, Mandie's mind was preoccupied with what a very mysterious person Grace Wilson was.

chapter 12

The next afternoon Mandie and her friends were not able to return to the flower shop as they had promised Grace, because Senator Morton unexpectedly arrived in Charleston to "check on the girls" for Mrs. Taft. She was concerned about the ghost story and the fact that Mandie and Celia were staying with the Dunnigans and not in their room at the boardinghouse.

Senator Morton was already at the Dunnigans' when the girls came home from classes.

"I had to come through here on my way back to Washington and promised your grandmother I would look in on you to be sure everything was all right," he told Mandie as everyone sat in the Dunnigans' parlor. He smiled at Mandie and added, "You know how she worries about you."

"And she doesn't have a thing to worry about concerning me. In fact, Celia and Mary Lou and I are in the middle of an investigation into this tale about the ghost," Mandie replied.

"Well, well, young lady, you are still finding mysteries to solve, aren't you?" Senator Morton said, returning her smile.

"We think we are about to solve this one," Mandie replied matter-of-factly. She related the events to date, then added, "And as soon as we can get into the locksmith's old records, I believe we will find the answer to the puzzle."

"Now, I'm not being nosy myself, but are you and Miss Celia planning to move back into your room at the boardinghouse after you solve this mystery?" the senator asked.

"Eventually we'll move back into our room, but I really like it here," Mandie replied with a big grin as she looked at Mr. and Mrs. Dunnigan.

"And you both are most welcome here, and we expect you to stay the rest of the school year at least with us," Mrs. Dunnigan quickly said, as much for the girls' benefit as for the senator's.

"Oh, thank you, Mrs. Dunnigan," Celia told her. "We're so grateful for your kind hospitality. I wish we could stay until we graduate."

"Then stay you must," Mrs. Dunnigan told her and Mandie. Looking at the senator, she added, "I told the girls it is wonderful having them here, since Mary Lou is an only child."

"That's so very kind of you, Mrs. Dunnigan," the senator said.

"Oh, Senator Morton, would you please deliver a message from me to my grandmother?" Mandie asked.

"Of course."

"Please let her know that everyone is coming to my house for the spring holidays, so I'm sure she will want to be there, too."

"I'm afraid your grandmother may be one step ahead of you,"

Senator Morton said, clearing his throat. "She is already making plans to come to your house, because she figured everyone will be there to see the new babies."

"One of these days I hope to get a little ahead of her," Mandie said. Smiling, she added, "You know what I mean, Senator."

The senator laughed as he said, "Yes, your grandmother is a wonderful lady. She knows right where to be, and she always manages to get there early."

Mandie suddenly remembered the remark the bookstore owner had made to her grandmother back in the fall. She drew a deep breath and asked, "You were a friend of my grandfather, weren't you?"

"He and I grew up together and we were indeed great friends," he answered.

"Well, can you tell me what happened to him?" Mandie asked, closely watching the senator. "You see, he died so many years ago and I never knew him."

"Your grandfather died from an accident, dear," Senator Morton answered. "However, please don't ask me for details, because that is something your grandmother refuses to discuss."

"But why? Why all the secrecy?" Mandie asked. "I overheard a woman in a bookstore downtown tell my grandmother that she read about it in all the newspapers. Evidently something out of the ordinary happened."

"I'm sorry, Miss Amanda, but that is where I have to draw the line," Senator Morton replied with a sad expression on his face.

"Now, tell me about your college. Are you enjoying your classes there?"

Mandie took another deep breath to control her anger. Why was everyone so secretive about her grandfather's death? She would find out for herself one day. In the meantime, she tried to smile as she said, "Yes, sir, I am learning a lot about money. I suppose that's the main reason I'm here, because my grandmother insisted I needed to learn all this." Then Mandie leaned forward to whisper, "But she doesn't know I will give all that money away if I do inherit it someday. I can't be bothered to look after such stuff when there are so many other pleasant things in life to do."

"Well, Miss Amanda, what are you planning to do?" Senator Morton asked with an alarmed expression on his face.

"I might just rent me an office after I finish school, hang out a sign in front that says *Amanda Shaw, Lady Detective,* or maybe I'll just take over the orphanage that Joe and I founded and run it. I definitely don't want to be burdened with money like my grandmother is."

Senator Morton gave a pleased grin and said, "Rest assured I will not give away your secret."

Mary Lou spoke up. "But, Mandie, you wouldn't have to handle the money yourself. That's the kind of business my father is in. Other people could do it for you, and then you could still be a detective."

"You're right, that is the kind of business I'm in, but I don't have any clients with large fortunes to handle," Mr. Dunnigan said with a laugh.

"Joe Woodard has asked several times to handle the money for you," Celia reminded her.

Mandie cleared her throat and firmly repeated, "I may never get married." Turning back to the senator she asked, "How long will you be here? I'd be glad to show you our college if you have time."

"Thank you, dear, but I must get the train tomorrow to continue on my way. We have several votes coming up in the senate that I don't want to miss," Senator Morton replied. "Perhaps another time I will be coming through and have more time."

Mrs. Dunnigan spoke from across the room. "We insist that you stay tonight with us, rather than in that hotel, Senator. We have plenty of room."

"Thank you very much, Mrs. Dunnigan. If I won't be imposing on y'all, I would be most happy to stay," the senator said.

"And I would like for you to see the boardinghouse and meet Mrs. Thomason," Mandie said. "She can tell you all about this ghost tale, and then you can relay it to my grandmother."

"I would like to see the boardinghouse and meet Mrs. Thomason. I know your grandmother will be asking all about it," Senator Morton said. "I'll be stopping over in Asheville on my way to Washington, so I will talk to her then," he explained.

When the men went to pick up the senator's baggage, Mrs. Dunnigan worked on supper and the girls went upstairs to Mandie and Celia's room to discuss their changed plans for the day.

Mandie sighed and said, "Grandmother seems to know how to disrupt everything even when she's not present. I'm wondering what Grace will think when we don't come back this afternoon."

"I don't think she'll worry about it. She will know something delayed us." Mary Lou comforted Mandie's thoughts.

"We'll just be sure to go tomorrow afternoon," Celia added.

"I wish Senator Morton would have told me about my grandfather," Mandie said. "There seems to be some deep, dark secret concerning his death. No one will ever talk about it."

Mary Lou suddenly straightened as she said, "Mandie, have you ever thought about searching the records yourself to see what happened? After all, your grandfather was a United States senator—an important man."

"And evidently the newspapers all wrote about it," Celia added. "Remember what that lady said in the bookstore down on Meeting Street that day?"

"But where would the records be? In Washington, D.C.? I would never be able to go up there—not without my grandmother or mother—so how could I even see the records?" Mandie asked.

"Too bad you didn't know about this when you were in Washington for President McKinley's inauguration that time," Celia said.

"Yes, I know," Mandie said. Then she frowned and added, "I don't understand why so many people have to keep secrets from me. You don't know this, Mary Lou, but I didn't even know my real mother until my father died when I was eleven years old.

And I didn't know that I was one-fourth Cherokee until after my father died and Uncle Ned told me."

Mary Lou gasped in surprise.

"I think it's just awful that everyone kept all that from you," Celia said, sounding angry.

"Since people always seem to be keeping secrets from you, I wonder if there is anything else they haven't told you," Mary Lou wondered aloud.

"I certainly hope not," Mandie said. "I'm all grown up now and want to be treated as such."

"Then let's figure out a way that we can go to Washington and get into the records about your grandfather," Mary Lou suggested.

Mandie looked at her friend and said, "Mary Lou, there is no way I can get away from my grandmother, my mother, *and* Uncle John to go to Washington. And if any of them agree to come with us, they would never let us search the records, because they're all trying so hard to keep that a secret from me."

"Don't give up on it," Celia said sympathetically. Then an idea seemed to come to her as she brightened and said, "We might be able to arrange for my mother to escort us if we don't tell her exactly what our plans are. I'm sure if we said we'd just like to visit the National Archives, she'd think we were interested in history in general."

Mandie's eyes widened as she looked at her friend and said, "That may be a possibility. Why don't you talk to your mother, Celia. In the meantime, while we're here, we need to solve this ghost mystery for Mrs. Thomason."

After supper that night the girls walked with Senator Morton around the block to see Mrs. Thomason. She was surprised to meet the senator.

"Let's sit in my private parlor and we'll have Sadie bring us coffee and cakes, shall we?" she said, leading the way.

They found seats in the small room while Mrs. Thomason went to order refreshments. She soon returned with Sadie pushing the tea cart.

"This is a pleasure, Senator Morton," Mrs. Thomason said as everyone was served. "I have heard so much about you."

Senator Morton laughed and said, "Well, I do hope it was all good."

"Yes, indeed," Mrs. Thomason said with a slightly embarrassed laugh. "I've followed some of your decisions made on votes in Washington. You see, our local newspaper covers most of the political scene in Washington."

"I'm glad to hear that," the senator said, sipping his coffee.

Then Mrs. Thomason turned to the girls. "I hear you three have been back to the flower shop. Were you able to get any information about the keys?"

"Not yet," Mandie answered. "We will probably go back down there tomorrow afternoon. I'm hoping we can get into the old papers the locksmith left when he moved out of the shop."

"I wish I could go with you, but business is picking up right now—and I can't leave Sadie alone, either," Mrs. Thomason said quickly. Turning to the senator, she explained the story of Sadie's ghost sighting. "I'm sure there is an explanation, and we're trying to find it."

"Down in Florida, where I live, people claim to see ghosts sometimes in the swamps," Senator Morton told Mrs. Thomason. "And in old graveyards and such."

"Oh dear, have *you* ever seen a ghost, Senator Morton?" Mrs. Thomason asked with a skeptical look on her face.

"No, ma'am, I have not," he said. "However, some of the stories about ghosts, especially around St. Augustine, just can't seem to be explained. A lot of people down there do believe in ghosts."

Turning back to the girls, Mrs. Thomason said, "When you get a chance to look through those papers at the flower shop, please let me know if you find the boardinghouse address on anything. If the locksmith kept careful records, a name should appear with the address, and from that I can hopefully see whether the name is someone who lived here or not."

"Mrs. Poinsett packed all the papers up when she took over the building, so there ought to be some kind of records there," Mandie said. "I can't imagine what could be on a pile of papers except his business dealings."

"Then maybe we will be able to find something that will help us," Mary Lou said.

"I hope we can get to the bottom of this rather soon. It's been very unsettling," Mrs. Thomason told them.

The girls assured her that they wouldn't quit until the mystery of the ghost was solved.

The next afternoon, when they went back to the flower shop, they discovered that Grace had obtained permission from Mrs. Poinsett to go through the old papers, and the girls set to work in a hurry.

Mandie kept flipping papers, trying to read the handwriting on each one, then finally declared, "These papers are all written in a foreign language of some kind. Look at this. None of them are readable." She sighed as she shuffled the papers on the counter where they had emptied out a box.

Celia, Mary Lou, and Grace gathered around to look.

"Is it the handwriting that is illegible maybe?" Grace asked.

"Or is it some kind of code?" Celia asked.

"The numbers on these are legible, but not the rest of the writing," Mary Lou declared as she shifted the ones she had on the counter.

Looking at Grace, she asked, "Do you know if Mr. Jacks was a foreigner and wrote in another language?"

Grace shook her head and said, "I never met him."

Mandie looked at Mary Lou and said, "Your father said he talked to the man. He didn't say anything about him being a foreigner, did he?"

"Not that I remember," Mary Lou replied, still shuffling through the papers.

Celia suddenly realized something. "I don't believe the man was a foreigner. I think he must have been uneducated and didn't know how to spell or write, so he had his own code to record things."

The girls looked closely at the papers again. The series of symbols did seem to be in repetitive patterns.

"Oh goodness. How can we ever decipher such stuff?" Mandie asked.

"Here's one where he has drawn a diagram or map showing someone's house or building," Grace said, waving a paper in front of her.

The girls scanned the paper.

Mary Lou suddenly said, "I believe I can figure that one out. That's a house at the corner of Adair and Leslie Streets. See the way he drew the crooked roads. And Leslie is a dead end."

"You are right," Mandie agreed. "I don't know the street names, but I can tell this is supposed to be roadways of some kind."

"If that's what he has done, it will take hours and hours to decipher all these addresses," Celia complained. "And you would have to do most of it, Mary Lou, because we don't know the streets in Charleston like you do."

"If only my father could look at these papers. He would know so much better than I do about the streets," Mary Lou said.

"Maybe I could get permission from Mrs. Poinsett for y'all to take the papers to your house, Mary Lou," Grace volunteered. "Do you think your father would have time to look through these?"

"Oh yes, I'm sure he'd take time to help us out," Mary Lou

said. "And Mrs. Thomason might be able to help, too."

"Then I'll ask Mrs. Poinsett tonight about doing that," Grace promised.

"This sure is taking a long time," Celia complained. "I wish there was some way to speed things up so we could figure out whether Sadie really saw a ghost or not."

"I'm sure Sadie did not see a ghost. That's why we're going through these papers—to find out who could have played a trick on her, remember?" Mandie said, stuffing papers back into the boxes.

"Well, whether y'all believe in ghosts or not, I noticed Senator Morton never did say he *didn't* believe in ghosts. Did y'all notice that?" Celia asked.

Mandie frowned as she thought about his conversation. "Yes, you're right."

"I think we'd better get going or we may be late for supper," Mary Lou reminded the girls. They all said good-bye, with Grace promising to get permission for them to take boxes home with them to get help going through the papers.

Later, when everyone was sitting at the supper table, Mary Lou explained to her father what they would like to do. "We think the papers all have diagrams and drawings on them."

"I wouldn't be at all surprised; I don't believe that man could read or write," Mr. Dunnigan replied. "I'd be glad to look at the papers for y'all."

"Should we ask Mrs. Thomason to look at the papers, also?" Mrs. Dunnigan asked. "She would be looking for her house and might recognize whatever scrawling the man might have made for it."

"Yes, that is a very good idea," Mr. Dunnigan replied. "Would you find out if she might be able to get together with us tomorrow night?"

"I'll find out," Mrs. Dunnigan promised.

After supper the three girls got together in Mandie and Celia's room for their nightly rehash of the day's events.

"You know, I've been thinking about this search," Mandie said, settling into one of the big chairs. "What if it turns out to be someone we know?"

"Well, we wouldn't have to confront them ourselves. Mrs. Thomason can take care of all that," Celia said, flopping on the bed.

Mary Lou straightened up in her chair and said, "I sure hope it's not someone we think is a friend. That could be embarrassing."

"I wonder what Mrs. Thomason will do about it if we do find out who is involved," Mandie said.

"Well, I don't know what she will do, but I know what I would do," Mary Lou said. "I'd contact the newspaper and have them print an embarrassing story about what a stupid trick they did."

Mandie suddenly sat up straight and gasped. "Oh goodness! I hadn't even thought about it, but you know what might happen? Suppose Senator Morton mentioned to someone that we were looking for a ghost? The newspapers print everything he says because he's a politician. That would be absolutely terrible. I wish we had not told him anything about this ghost business at all."

Mary Lou laughed and said, "That might be fun, getting our names in the paper because we are chasing ghosts!"

"My grandmother wouldn't like that at all," Mandie declared.

"I don't think I'd want my name in the newspaper connected with ghosts," Celia said with a shiver.

"And just imagine what those fellows around the college would say if we solved the mystery of the haunted boardinghouse," Mary Lou said.

Mandie laughed and said, "Then they wouldn't have anything to talk about!"

Mandie knew she would keep investigating the mystery until they discovered an answer—even if it took the whole year to do it.

chapter 13

The next afternoon Mandie and her friends went back to the flower shop and, with Mrs. Poinsett's permission, brought home three boxes of the papers. Mrs. Thomason had asked them to come over to her house with the papers after supper.

"Oh dear, these papers are a frightful mess, aren't they?" Mrs. Thomason said as she began sorting through them on the dining room table. Supper had already been served to her boarders, so the room was clear for the night.

"I believe these are diagrams of different houses and different streets, but there are no names indicating the streets or anyone's house," Mr. Dunnigan said.

"I don't see what good these papers were to him," Mrs. Dunnigan said, flipping through another stack of papers.

"He didn't even put the cost or the price charged on any of these," Mandie said.

"Now that you mention it, when I got him to make my new lock and key, he didn't seem able to add up money. He just gave me a rounded figure for what I owed him," Mrs. Thomason told the others.

Mr. Dunnigan paused in his work and looked at the girls. "Are these all of the papers?"

Mandie shook her head. "No, Grace said that they had stored his papers in the attic and in the basement. We carried these up from the basement, so there are still papers left in the attic."

"We'll have to look at those when we take these back," Mary Lou said.

"Well, I'm finding that I can recognize quite a few of these houses, according to his diagrams," Mrs. Thomason said. "But we don't even know what all of these houses mean."

They searched all the papers but found nothing else, then declared it a night.

"Such a waste of time, both for Mr. Jacks and for anyone trying to find a particular record," Mr. Dunnigan said about the locksmith's record-keeping.

"We can go back and look at the other papers tomorrow afternoon," Mandie promised.

The next afternoon the three girls hurried back to the flower shop with the boxes of papers they had already looked through. Grace saw them coming and quickly met them at the door.

"Please come in," she said anxiously. "The man has been here demanding his papers, and I had to tell him someone had borrowed some of them. I did not say who, but he took all of his boxes out of the attic."

"Sol Jacks was back? But Mr. Dunnigan said he left as a crew

MANDIE ✦ HER COLLEGE DAYS

member on a ship before Christmas," Mandie said.

"The ship must have already come back to port," Mary Lou concluded.

"And why would he come back to the flower shop for papers that he left behind for garbage?" Celia asked. "They could have been long gone by now."

"What did he look like?" Mary Lou asked. "My father has seen him before, so he would know if the man who came here and got the papers was really the locksmith."

"Good point. We should ask your father about him," Mandie said to Mary Lou. Then it was apparent another idea dawned on her. "But why would anyone else want all that garbage?"

"Mr. Jacks claimed he had intended coming back to get the papers, but he had to leave immediately on that ship or lose his job," Grace said. "He was a small man, slender and not very tall, possibly in his fifties."

"But his lease was up when he left, according to my father, so how could he expect to come back and get papers that he left in a place that he no longer paid rent on?" Mary Lou said.

"What did you tell him about the rest of his papers?" Celia asked Grace.

"I only said that they had been borrowed—I did not give him any information other than that. In fact, I was a little afraid of him, but thankfully some customers came in, so he quickly left, saying he would return for the balance of his papers."

"You need someone to stay here with you. The man might be dangerous if he finds you alone," Mandie said.

"When Mrs. Poinsett comes in I'll discuss it with her. She has a grandson who helps out now and then, so maybe he will stay here with me until all this commotion dies down," Grace said.

"I'll talk to my father about this and see what he thinks," Mary Lou told her. "I don't believe that man could have gone off on a ship and gotten back this fast. Besides, why did the papers become so important to him all of a sudden?"

Grace glanced at the boxes and shrugged. "Well, did y'all find any information about his work in those papers?"

"No, just some rough drawings of houses and streets," Mary Lou replied. "Some we could understand, but most of it was just jumbled drawings."

"It's too bad we didn't get a chance to go through the other boxes," Mandie said. "They probably contained more information, maybe even names of clients."

"Why doesn't one of us stay here with you until Mrs. Poinsett comes?" Mary Lou offered. "I'll wait here with you while Mandie and Celia go back to my house and let my parents know what we are doing."

"Thank you, but I'll be all right. I'll ask Mr. Perry in the pottery shop next door to keep an eye out for me," Grace replied.

"Why don't you keep the door locked until Mrs. Poinsett comes? You can see through the window if any customers are at the door, and if that man comes back, then don't open it," Mandie suggested.

"That's a good idea. I will lock it when y'all leave," Grace said.

"I hope we catch up with you in chapel tomorrow morning

and find out if anything else happened after we left," Mary Lou told her.

"I'll look for y'all there," Grace promised, following them to the door and smiling through the glass as she locked the door behind them.

When the girls got back to the Dunnigans' house, Mr. Dunnigan was already home, and the girls related the events to him and Mrs. Dunnigan.

"It sounds like Sol Jacks never got on the boat. It would be impossible for him to sail off like that and return so soon afterward," Mr. Dunnigan said.

Mary Lou gave her father the description of the man that Grace had given them. "Do you think it was really the locksmith who came after the papers? Would that description fit him?"

"Yes, that does sound like what I remember of him," Mr. Dunnigan replied. "But there is something very strange about all this. He left the shop in a big hurry all those months ago, and he left the papers in it—for garbage. Now he's returning to collect them when he doesn't even rent the shop anymore? I don't understand what is going on."

The girls walked out to Mrs. Thomason's boardinghouse and told her about the episode concerning the man. She also agreed that the desciption fit the man. Mrs. Thomason warned the girls to stay out of trouble.

The next morning the girls found Grace in the chapel early enough to talk for a few minutes.

"Did he come back?" Mandie asked Grace as they sat down next to her.

"He did, but he didn't get any more papers," Grace replied with a big smile. "Mrs. Poinsett was so upset with this that she gave all the remaining papers to Mr. Perry next door and told him to hide them away somewhere, that the man had no right to come back and demand the papers he left for garbage—in a shop he no longer rented."

"What a smart woman," Mary Lou said, amazed at the older woman's ferocity.

"So what happened when she refused to give him the papers?" Celia asked.

"She didn't tell him she had given the papers to Mr. Perry. She just said everything he had left there had been thrown out and there was nothing belonging to him left, and not to come back anymore," Grace explained.

"I don't imagine he liked that," Mandie said.

"No, but when Mrs. Poinsett told him she would ask the law to take him to jail, he left in a hurry," Grace explained.

"So now we'll never know whether someone had him duplicate a key to Mrs. Thomason's house," Mandie said with a sigh.

"No, we'll just have to think up another angle," Mary Lou said.

——————

No one had uncovered any more information about the so-called ghost in the boardinghouse or about Sol Jacks, and suddenly it was time for the spring holidays. Mandie, Celia, and Mary Lou were excited to be spending the time together at Mandie's house. The Shaws' house was full once again as several people met there for this holiday, including Jonathan Guyer and his father, Lindall Guyer, who had once been in love with Mandie's grandmother; Senator Morton, who seemed to currently consider Mrs. Taft the apple of his eye; Joe Woodard, who was on his spring break from his college in New Orleans, and his parents, Dr. and Mrs. Woodard; Uncle Ned and his wife, Morningstar, and their granddaughter, Sallie; Mandie's grandmother; and Celia's mother, Jane Hamilton. At the last minute, Celia's old friend Robert, from Mr. Chadwick's School for Boys in Asheville, North Carolina, came.

The twin babies, Carol and Carl, were growing and alert to all the attention bestowed on them.

Although everyone was kept busy with little time to eat and sleep, the days flew by and they soon had to return to their various places.

Back at their college, Mandie, Celia, and Mary Lou learned that Grace had worked most of the holiday, alongside Mrs. Poinsett's grandson, Matthew, who was also on holiday from the College of Charleston. Mandie remarked to Celia and Mary Lou that Matthew seemed infatuated with Grace and was using the excuse of tending shop in order to be around her.

"That could be an interesting matter," Mary Lou said to Mandie and Celia after they had visited the shop one afternoon.

"Yes, I noticed the way his attention stayed with Grace

instead of with the customers," Celia said.

"I can't tell whether it's mutual or not," Mandie said. "I noticed that Grace did not talk to him very much."

"Maybe she's just shy around boys," Celia said.

"Or it could be that Grace wants to go ahead with her career and not get sidetracked," Mandie said.

On Monday morning, when the girls came down for breakfast before leaving for school, Mr. and Mrs. Dunnigan were discussing something in the morning newspaper.

"If it's not one of those houses, then it's awfully close to it," Mr. Dunnigan was saying. Looking up as the girls came into the room, he told them, "There was a burglary in a house not far from here over the weekend, and I'd say it seems to be a house that Sol Jacks drew on one of his papers." He handed Mary Lou the newspaper to look at the picture of the house involved.

"Why, it does seem to be one of those houses," Mary Lou said in surprise. "Do you suppose the locksmith is involved in this?"

"That's what I've been asking myself," her father replied. "There's something about that man that doesn't ring true. And you will notice the article says it was not a forced entry. Whoever did it had a key to get in."

"Will you be talking to the law authorities about this?" Mrs. Dunnigan asked her husband.

"Well, I suppose I should," he replied thoughtfully. "Of course, we don't have any of those papers left to show them and explain."

"But, Papa, Mrs. Poinsett does have some of the papers," Mary

Lou reminded him. "Remember, Grace said Mrs. Poinsett gave the papers to Mr. Perry in the shop next door to keep for her?"

"You are right," Mr. Dunnigan said with a smile. "I'll go down there today and look over whatever Mr. Perry is keeping. Then I'll know whether it would be worthwhile to mention this to the law enforcement officers.

When the girls came home from their classes that day, Mr. Dunnigan was excited to tell them what he had discovered that morning.

"Y'all were right about those papers. I spoke with Mrs. Poinsett this morning, and she had already considered Sol Jacks's connection to the burglary. So we got the papers from the pottery shop owner and went over them. We believe we found a diagram of the house that was burglarized."

"What did you do with it?" Mary Lou asked excitedly.

"With Mrs. Poinsett's permission, I took it to the law enforcement office. They were so impressed with the drawing, they asked to see the rest of the papers. They've now set up surveillance on the other houses in the diagrams," Mr. Dunnigan explained. "I believe we have helped prevent other burglaries."

"I do hope so," Mrs. Dunnigan said.

"Do you know whether one of the houses in the drawings was Mrs. Thomason's boardinghouse?" Mandie asked.

"We don't think so," Mr. Dunnigan said. "More than likely her house is on the other papers we haven't been able to see. I plan to change the locks on this house and my office as soon as another locksmith can get to it. In the meantime I will leave lights burning at night when I close up."

"Papa, you shouldn't have to change the lock on your office. It's so near the law enforcement office, and I don't think the man would dare bother it right under their noses," Mary Lou said.

"I don't trust that man, Mary Lou," Mr. Dunnigan replied. "I believe he would dare to do anything that came to his mind."

"Mrs. Thomason was having her locks on the boardinghouse changed today," Mrs. Dunnigan assured the girls, "and said she would bring you girls new keys so you can get in."

Mary Lou looked at Mandie and Celia and said, "I don't know why y'all don't just move your things out of her house and into ours. Y'all aren't going to stay there for the rest of the school year, anyhow."

Mrs. Dunnigan spoke up. "Yes, that's what I was thinking, too. Why don't y'all just give up your room over there? I've told you already you are both welcome here. In fact, you seem like part of our family now and we wouldn't want y'all to move out."

Mandie and Celia looked at each other. Celia shrugged her shoulders. Mandie smiled and looked at Mrs. Dunnigan. "Thank you, Mrs. Dunnigan, we appreciate your kindness so much. Celia and I love living here with y'all and don't really want to go back to the boardinghouse. I guess we should just move the rest of our things over here then."

"When Mr. Ryland comes to take us to the flower shop, why don't we just get him to move our things then?" Celia suggested to Mandie. "It won't take long because we don't have much left over there."

"Yes, we can do that and get everything settled once and for all," Mandie answered.

"I'm so glad y'all are going to stay with us for the rest of the school year. It would be awfully lonely around here without y'all, now that we've gotten so used to each other," Mary Lou said with a big smile.

Mr. Ryland was waiting with the carriage when everyone finished the noonday meal, and they all went over to Mrs. Thomason's house.

"Well, welcome, all of you," Mrs. Thomason said, opening the door in surprise to see Mr. and Mrs. Dunnigan along with Mandie, Celia, and Mary Lou.

"Mrs. Thomason, we've decided to move the rest of our things over to the Dunnigans'," Mandie quickly explained. "Our school year will be over soon anyhow, and it will give you a chance to rent our room to someone who might be more permanent."

"I understand," Mrs. Thomason said, nodding. "Perhaps next school year you girls will want a room here again."

"Perhaps," Mandie replied. "But right now things have been so frightening and hectic that I don't believe we would even sleep at night if we were to stay here."

"I know exactly what you mean, dear," Mrs. Thomason replied. "However, I should let you know that I did have all the locks changed on my house today and was preparing to give y'all new keys. I feel everything here is safe now."

"That is good to know," Mandie said.

"Mr. Ryland is waiting to load their things into the carriage,"

Mr. Dunnigan told Mrs. Thomason. "Shall I ask him to come inside now?"

"Yes, please do," Mrs. Thomason replied.

With the small amount of belongings Mandie and Celia had left at the boardinghouse, the two men had the room emptied and the carriage loaded in just a short while. Mr. Dunnigan surveyed the carriage, then looked at the girls and said, "Well, even so, we managed to fill the carriage and there is no room for anyone to ride, so we should start walking back so we can let Mr. Ryland into the house with your things."

"Yes, sir," Mandie and Celia agreed.

As everyone said good-bye to Mrs. Thomason, she suddenly called to Mandie. "Oh dear, Amanda, I almost forgot. Please wait a minute. You received some mail today that I need to give you." She hurried back inside the house as everyone waited on the walkway.

"I wonder who wrote to me at this house." Mandie looked puzzled.

Then Mrs. Thomason came back to the door with a small white envelope in her hand. "It must be important. I noticed it came all the way from Ireland," she said.

"Adrian," Mandie said under her breath. She took the white envelope and quickly slipped it into the pocket of her full skirt.

Celia heard her and grinned. "Adrian. He won't give up, will he?"

Mary Lou grinned at Mandie and teased, "Oh, a beau in Ireland!"

Mr. and Mrs. Dunnigan overheard the remarks and smiled as everyone headed back toward the Dunnigans'.

It didn't take long for Mr. Dunnigan and Mr. Ryland to get the carriage unloaded, and with Mary Lou's help, the girls soon had all their clothes hung up and everything in place.

"Now, shall we go to the flower shop?" Mary Lou asked.

"I would like to freshen up a little before we go," Mandie told her friends. "I'll only be a minute or two." She headed down the hallway toward the bathroom.

"It should only take two minutes at the most to open that letter and read it," Mary Lou teased.

"We'll be down in the parlor," Celia called to Mandie. She couldn't keep the grin off her face.

In the bathroom, Mandie quickly opened the letter and pulled out the one sheet of paper. She read, *Just a note to let you know that I shall be sailing for America shortly and will spend some time in your city. I do hope you will be remaining in Charleston for the summer. Upon arrival I shall contact you at your college. Until then, Adrian.*

Mandie straightened up and said to herself, "I hope you don't get here before I go home for the summer. I doubt that you'd ever find me in my little hometown in North Carolina." She quickly stuck the letter back inside the envelope, rushed into her room, and buried it in her pile of scarves and ribbons in the bureau drawer.

As she hurried down the stairs to join her friends, she muttered to herself, "Too many things happening at once."

Mandie wasn't sure whether she wanted to see Adrian when he came to the United States or not. He had seemed interesting when she had met him in Europe last summer, but that was a long time ago, and they didn't seem to have much in common.

"Oh well, I have plenty of time to decide about that. School won't be out for a while yet."

Rushing into the parlor, she felt herself blush when Mary Lou and Celia grinned at her.

"Come on, let's go," she said, continuing to walk toward the front door. "We don't have a whole lot of time left today."

Mary Lou and Celia smiled at each other and hurried after her.

chapter 1 4

The next day the newspaper published an article about the burglaries that had been happening around town. It mentioned Sol Jacks as a suspect, since he had apparently been into some questionable dealings recently, and how he had suddenly fled town.

Mandie, Celia, and Mary Lou read the article together at breakfast that morning.

"He jumped onto a boat bound for Africa?" Mandie was both shocked and angry. "Now the police will never be able to catch him!"

"Well, at least we won't have to worry about him using those diagrams he still has to break into more houses," Celia said.

And with the absence of Sol Jacks came the absence of burglaries. The law officials decided that the locksmith was indeed their guilty man.

The school year neared the end. There were concerts, lectures, and out-of-town visitors speaking on various topics; and the worry about final examinations began to spread among the girls.

Both Mary Lou and Grace had strict standards they had to meet in order to receive an extension on their scholarships for the next year. And Mandie, Celia, Mary Lou, and Grace often studied together on subjects they were taking.

The other girls at the college were still aloof and hostile with them at times. George Stuart's sister continued staring and smirking at Mandie whenever she saw her. April Snow and Polly Cornwallis just ignored Mandie and Celia and Mary Lou.

One day Mandie wanted to look at books at the antique bookstore and Celia went with her. Mary Lou and Grace had to stay behind to study for their final exams. Mandie promised to pick up Mary Lou at four o'clock.

On their way to Meeting Street, Celia remarked, "You know, Mandie, this would be an opportunity to ask the bookstore owner questions about your grandfather."

"Don't you remember? We tried that before and it didn't work," Mandie replied.

"Do you think there's a possibility she might have old newspapers in her shop?" Celia asked.

"I had not thought about that," Mandie replied. "I don't remember seeing anything but books there, but we could ask Mrs. Heyward if she keeps any old newspapers."

When they entered the shop, Mrs. Heyward was busy talking to an elderly lady. "That's a question I get very often, but I'm sorry to say that we don't keep any old newspapers. They are too much trouble. However, you can go to the newspaper office and look at every paper they have ever put out."

"I thank you for the information," the lady said, looking around. "I'll just take a look at your books, then."

Mandie and Celia also looked at the books on the shelves, but Mandie was so deep in thought that she only pretended to see the books in front of her. "I wonder where the newspaper office is," she finally whispered to Celia.

"Mrs. Heyward could probably tell us, if you want to ask," Celia replied.

"No, I'd rather ask Mr. Ryland. I'm sure he would know," Mandie said.

"And I'm sure he could take us there," Celia added.

"If we go right now, we'll have time to stop in the newspaper office before we have to pick Mary Lou up from the college," Mandie said. "Come on, I'll look for a book some other time."

They hurried outside to where Mr. Ryland was waiting with the carriage.

"Mr. Ryland, do you know where the newspaper office is?" Mandie asked as they approached him.

"Oh sure. Do you want to go there?" Mr. Ryland replied.

"Yes, sir, I'd like to look up some old newspapers concerning something I heard about," Mandie explained.

"Then we go," he said.

The newspaper building was tall and slender, three stories high, and stood between a dry goods store and a hardware store. Mandie looked up at it and asked, "Mr. Ryland, does the newspaper use the whole building?"

"Oh yes, miss, they do. You see, they've been here a long time, and they save every newspaper they've ever printed. It takes a big building to hold all of it," he replied as they stood by the carriage.

"Would you please wait for us while we're in there?" Mandie asked. "We shouldn't be too long."

"Certainly, miss, I'll be right here," he replied.

Mandie and Celia pushed open the heavy front door and found themselves in a large room, most of which was fenced off by a large counter at the front. They could see several desks where people sat working on papers. One man was hollering over a telephone in an effort to be heard on the other end of the line. Two men were standing in the far back corner of the room, evidently arguing loudly with hands waving, enforcing whatever was being said.

Mandie looked at Celia as they stood at the counter. "What do we do now, I wonder? No one seems to have noticed us come in."

"If we could get past this counter, we could probably get someone's attention," Celia said, looking around for an opening.

The two men standing in the back stopped talking, and one came toward the front but stopped before he got to the counter. He looked up and saw the girls and then walked away, ignoring them.

"Well, how do you like that?" Mandie said. She suddenly raised her voice and yelled, "Mister, we have a question."

The discussions in the room stopped immediately and everyone stared at the two girls, but no one came forward.

"Please, could we speak to someone?" Mandie said to no one in particular.

The man who had started forward before finally came to the counter. "What do you ladies want?" he asked in a harsh voice.

"We would like to ask about looking at copies of old newspapers, please," Mandie said, trying to sound older so they wouldn't ignore her again.

"You want to look at old newspapers?" the man replied. "No way, miss, not today. We are in the process of putting the paper to bed and don't have time. Come back another day." He started to walk away from the counter.

"If you would just show us where they are, we won't bother you," Mandie said, determined to get into the papers.

"I'm sorry, miss, but you cannot get into the archives without someone supervising, and I said we're too busy today," the man said. "Now scram, get out of here."

Mandie straightened her shoulders, pushed out her chin, and said, "I have never run into such a rude man before. We will leave so you can do your screaming at someone else."

Mandie and Celia were distinctly aware that they had become the center of attention in the room. So they quickly turned around and opened the front door to head outside as conversations began and everyone started talking at once again.

Mr. Ryland saw them coming and stepped forward. "Did you get to see whatever you wanted to see?" he asked.

"Oh no, we didn't see anything but a huge room full of

ill-mannered men," Mandie replied, and she related the events to him.

"They were just too busy to be bothered with us," Celia said when Mandie was done. "We can come back another day." The girls climbed into the carriage.

"Where to now, misses?" Mr. Ryland asked.

"I wonder if the library might have some old newspapers," Mandie said.

"Do you know where the public library is, Mr. Ryland?" Celia asked.

"The public library? I am not sure about that, miss," Mr. Ryland replied. "Perhaps we could drive around and you could watch for it."

Mandie flipped open the watch she wore on a chain around her neck. "We'd have time to find it before we have to pick up Mary Lou, but we won't be able to go inside and look at records."

"All right, let's at least find it," Celia said.

Mr. Ryland drove up and down streets, but the girls could not spot the public library.

"We might as well go on to the college and wait for Mary Lou. There's not enough time left to do anything else," Mandie said.

"Yes, miss," Mr. Ryland said, shaking the reins.

"Oh good, this time of day the parking spaces will be in the shade of the trees. It has turned out to be an awfully warm day, hasn't it?" Celia commented.

"It certainly has—in more ways than one," Mandie said with a little laugh.

As they came to the front of the college, Mandie leaned forward and said, "Look, there's one of those motorcars—and it's taking up several parking spaces."

"I wonder who it is driving that thing," Celia said.

"I do believe it's a young woman," Mandie said as they came closer.

"You're right," Celia replied. "Now, who can she be?"

"I don't know, but who does she think she is to take up so many parking spaces?" Mandie said disgustedly.

Mr. Ryland slowed their carriage down as they got closer, and then he came to a stop near the motorcar. He looked back at the girls.

"That woman should move her motorcar, Mr. Ryland. There is barely enough space for us to even park," Mandie said to him. Then, looking at the woman in the vehicle, she called out, "You have to move. There's not enough space."

"I have to move?" the woman replied, laughing. "I'll sit here all day if I want to."

Shocked, Mandie said, "No, you won't, either. If you don't move, I'll go inside the office and get someone to come out here and make you move."

Several other people were standing around and could hear the conversation. There was a lot of snickering.

Suddenly the motorcar lurched forward with a big roar, out of control.

Mr. Ryland's horse panicked and sped off with the carriage. Mr. Ryland lost control, and the carriage swerved into a rock

wall on the side of the road. There was a loud crash, and Mr.
Ryland was thrown from the carriage. Mandie was hit by the
debris and passed completely out. Celia quickly jerked up her long
skirts and jumped forward, trying to grab the reins.

"Whoa, boy, whoa, boy!" she called to the horse as she
tightened her hold on the reins. "Steady now, boy. Whoa, whoa,"
she called in a soothing voice. The horse slowed down, and she
managed to get him to stop. He was stomping his feet and
snorting.

She jumped down from the carriage, her skirts held high, and
raced to soothe the frightened horse as she managed to tie the
reins around a lamppost. Rushing back to the carriage she found
Mary Lou and Grace trying to help Mandie. Other people were
bending over Mr. Ryland as he lay unconscious on the road.

"Mandie! Mandie!" Celia cried, tears streaming down her face.
Her skirts were twisted and she had lost her hat.

"Celia, we need to get a doctor," Mary Lou said, quickly
looking around.

"Mr. Ryland looks like he's hurt pretty badly," Grace said.

The girls who had been standing around the motorcar began
fussing. "Mandie shouldn't have started all this arguing,
anyhow," one was saying.

"She thinks she can have her way about everything," a tall
girl said.

"It's all her fault," another one said.

Grace stood up and yelled back at the crowd. "It was not
her fault. I saw everything. I was standing right here. That

woman deliberately drove her motorcar into the carriage."

"Mandie's just a stuck-up snob who thinks she can buy anything she wants," one girl said. "She and her grandmother are snooty, filthy-rich people without a sense of decency."

Grace hastily approached the girl who said this. "Let me tell you one thing. Her grandmother gave me my scholarship or I wouldn't have been able to come to college here. And I pray for her every day because of it."

Mandie was groaning, but she was still unconscious as she lay in the carriage.

A young man pushed his way through the crowd, saying loudly, "Please let me through. I'm Dr. Zeager." He was carrying a medical bag and he quickly got to Mandie to examine her. "She needs to go to the hospital immediately. So does the man lying out there in the road." He stood up and sternly said, "Please stand back."

A man who was with him came through the crowd, picked up Mandie, and carried her to another carriage that had stopped in the road. Then he and the doctor picked up Mr. Ryland and put him in the carriage next to Mandie.

"We have to go with her," Celia screamed at the doctor through the noisy crowd.

At that moment another carriage had pulled up and stopped. Celia glanced at it and immediately recognized the driver as Mr. Donovan, the driver Mrs. Taft had originally tried to hire at the beginning of the school year. Celia called out, "Please, Mr. Donovan, can you take us to the hospital?"

Mr. Donovan hurried down from his carriage and came to help Celia out of the carriage. "Miss, what on earth has been going on here?" he asked. "Come quickly. We will follow the doctor."

"Mary Lou, Grace, come on!" Celia called to them, and they climbed into Mr. Donovan's carriage.

The doctor drove his carriage at a high rate of speed, and Mr. Donovan kept up with him. Celia tried to talk against the noise of the carriage to explain what happened.

"That motorcar was taking up too many parking spaces, and suddenly it just sped into our carriage, Mr. Donovan. Oh, I'm so worried about Mandie," she said as tears streamed down her face.

"And poor Mr. Ryland," Mary Lou added.

"I intend finding out who that woman was driving that motorcar and see that she is punished for it," Grace said firmly. "I also intend reporting those girls to the college for the remarks they were making."

"Oh, what about the carriage Mandie's grandmother bought for her and Celia? It was so damaged I don't believe it will run anymore. And we just left it in the street back there," Mary Lou said, trying to glance back.

"I saw some boys trying to move it out of the street," Grace said, trying to calm her friends down.

It was only a few blocks to the hospital, but it seemed like miles as Mandie and Mr. Ryland lay there unconscious. Finally the doctor turned the carriage through the gate and pulled up in front of a huge stone building.

Suddenly people from the hospital came running out and took

Mandie and Mr. Ryland inside. Grace, Celia, and Mary Lou followed but were stopped by a nurse in the front reception room.

"I am Rita, Dr. Zeager's nurse. I'm sorry, but you are not allowed to go inside until a doctor says you can. Please wait out here." She indicated a row of chairs against the wall. "I will let you know the condition of the patients as soon as possible." She hastily went through a door into the other part of the hospital.

Celia was crying and Mary Lou tried to console her.

"I need to let someone know about Mandie," Celia said. "Her mother doesn't have a phone, but I think her grandmother does. I just hate to get Mrs. Taft involved in this. I can imagine what will happen if she arrives."

"But you have to let someone know, Celia," Mary Lou said.

"I wish I could call my mother, but we don't have a phone at our house yet, either. We live on a horse farm way out in the country," Celia said.

"I thought you looked like you were experienced with horses when you took on the task of controlling that horse just now," Grace said.

Celia shivered as she said, "I haven't had anything to do with horses since one threw my father and killed him several years ago." Fresh tears streamed down her face.

"You saved Mandie's life, Celia, because you knew how to control a runaway horse," Mary Lou said, reaching to put an arm around her.

"I'm worried about her. We don't know how badly she is hurt,"

Celia said, beginning to shake all over.

Grace looked around, saw a stack of blankets on a shelf behind the counter, and got up to get one for Celia.

"Thank you," Celia said in a shaky voice.

They waited for what seemed to be hours before the doctor finally came out to speak to them.

"My staff and I have made a thorough examination of both patients," he said. "Mr. Ryland has come to and seems to be suffering from a broken arm, plus some cuts and bruises. At his age he is really lucky to have survived that fall from the carriage." He paused and cleared his throat. "Now, the young lady, Miss Shaw, is still unconscious and must be left here under observation."

"Oh no," Celia said in a shaky voice. "What is wrong with her, doctor?"

"She suffered a terrible blow on the head," Dr. Zeager replied. "But she is resting right now after the medication we gave her."

"I need to let her mother know," Celia said.

"Yes, you should definitely let her family know where she is," the doctor said. "Now, you girls are from the college, is this correct?"

"Yes, sir," Mary Lou said. "I'm Mary Lou Dunnigan. Celia Hamilton and Mandie live at my house. Grace Wilson here lives in the dormitory."

"Then why don't you young ladies go home and see what you can do about contacting Miss Shaw's relatives, and I will know where to find you if I need you." He started to go back through the door.

"What about Mr. Ryland?" Mary Lou asked. "Do we need to contact his family?"

"No, he has given us his information, so we will do that," the doctor replied.

"Thank you, Dr. Zeager," Celia said, rising and holding the blanket about her.

Mr. Donovan had waited outside with his carriage and the girls went out to give the news. He immediately offered to drive them anywhere they needed to go.

Since Celia badly needed to change her clothes, they all went to the Dunnigans' house. There they explained to the Dunnigans what had happened.

"I will help you contact Mandie's family," Mr. Dunnigan offered.

Celia explained about the lack of phones.

"We can still contact them through our law enforcement," Mr. Dunnigan said. "I'll go down and talk with them while you girls get cleaned up."

"Would you please leave Mandie's grandmother to the last to contact?" Celia asked Mr. Dunnigan in a shaky voice. "I know Mandie would rather have her stepfather, or even my mother, come if possible."

"I'll do my best," Mr. Dunnigan promised her as he left.

The girls went upstairs to clean up.

"Grace, why don't you just spend the night here with us?" Mary Lou asked.

"But I'm all dirty," Grace said, looking down at her dress.

"We look to be close to the same size. I think you could put on one of my dresses and it would fit well enough," Mary Lou said.

"All right then, but I do have a class first thing in the morning," Grace reminded her.

"Mr. Donovan said he would return tomorrow morning to see if he could take us anywhere," Celia reminded them, "so he can drive you back to school, Grace. I'm not going anywhere until I know how Mandie is going to be."

"Neither am I," Mary Lou added. "I want to be sure she's all right."

"I have to go in for that one class, but then I can come back," Grace said.

"Yes, please do," Mary Lou replied.

"I'll get some clothes, too," Grace said. "And I also want to talk to the people at the college and let them know what happened. I intend to follow through with this. Those girls were shouting lies about Mandie."

"Well, I hope they get some strong punishment," Celia said, her voice full of anger.

The three girls didn't sleep much that night. They talked awhile and then dozed, woke, and talked more. Celia gave them the verse she and Mandie always recited when in trouble or danger.

"Hold hands and say this: 'What time I am afraid, I will trust in thee,'" she explained.

The other girls joined in with her, and they finally drifted off to sleep just hours before sunrise.

chapter 15

Everyone was up early the next morning, after a night of restlessness. Mr. Donovan came by to take Grace back to the college, and then he returned to the Dunnigans' to be available if anyone else needed his carriage.

Mrs. Dunnigan invited him in for coffee, and as everyone sat around the table, Mr. Donovan told them that he had gone down to the carriage factory early that morning to check on the girls' carriage, as that is where it was taken after the accident. "It was completely destroyed," Mr. Donovan had to tell them.

"I talked to the law enforcement officer last night, and they promised to contact Mandie's family. I gave them some names and addresses, so I imagine we'll be hearing from someone soon," Mr. Dunnigan said.

"I need to go to the hospital and see about Mandie," Celia said in a shaky voice.

"They won't let you in, so you might as well wait here," Mary Lou reminded her. "I imagine Grace will find out something before she comes back here. And I imagine she will be making herself heard in that college today."

"In a way I hope Mrs. Taft will be the one contacted," Celia said. "She will really straighten out a few things if she shows up down here."

Finally there was a knock at the front door. The local law enforcement officer had come with news, so the Dunnigans invited him in for a cup of coffee.

"We were rather lucky," he said. "We sent a message in Morse code to the train depot in Franklin, North Carolina, and asked that they send it on to Mr. John Shaw, Miss Amanda Shaw's uncle. A reply came back that Mr. Shaw and his old Indian friend are on a hunting trip only a few miles from here. We sent a man out this morning in an effort to locate them. They will be told that there has been an accident and they should contact you immediately," the officer told Mr. Dunnigan.

"Oh, thank the Lord," Celia said under her breath. "I just know that Mr. Shaw will be here as soon as he gets the message."

"Is there anything else we can do?" the officer asked.

Mr. Dunnigan lowered his voice and tried to speak confidentially to the man. "I'm not sure what will happen at the college because of this accident. If it's left up to Mandie's grandmother, I'd say quite a bit will happen. That granddaughter is the apple of her eye."

"Of course we will enforce the law. We will do whatever is required of us," the officer said.

"Yes, I would insist that you do so," Mr. Dunnigan agreed.

Suddenly there was a pounding on the front door. Everyone jumped up as Mr. Dunnigan hurried to open it. Celia was right behind him.

As the door swung open, John Shaw and Uncle Ned appeared.

"What has happened?" John Shaw demanded.

"Come in, come in." Mr. Dunnigan motioned for the two men to enter, then closed the door behind them.

Everyone was quickly introduced while John Shaw and Uncle Ned looked around the room. "Where is Amanda?" John Shaw demanded.

"She's in the hospital," Mr. Dunnigan replied. "Please have seats for one minute while I explain."

As fast as he could speak, Mr. Dunnigan told them the story about what had happened yesterday morning.

John Shaw and Uncle Ned quickly stood and said, "Where is this hospital located?"

Mr. Donovan spoke as he reached for his hat from the hall tree. "Come with me. I will take you," he told the two men.

"Please let me go, too," Celia said.

"No, you stay here, Celia, because Mrs. Taft is on her way here right now," John Shaw said. "We will return shortly and let you know how things are." Without waiting for a reply, John Shaw quickly followed Mr. Donovan and Uncle Ned out the front door.

Everyone returned to the table to finish their coffee after the men left.

It wasn't long before Grace returned from the college, and Mary Lou insisted that they bring her up-to-date on their news before Grace could tell them what had happened at the college. "I'm so glad Mrs. Taft is coming," Grace said. "We may need her to straighten out that college. I talked to several officers, and no one seemed interested in doing anything about what happened. All those girls were in chapel this morning, but I didn't see the girl who was driving the motorcar—and the motorcar was nowhere to be seen. She must not be a student."

When Mr. Donovan brought John Shaw and Uncle Ned back from the hospital, Mrs. Taft was with them. She had come in on the train and gone straight to the hospital.

"Oh, do come in, Mrs. Taft," Mrs. Dunnigan greeted her at the door.

Mrs. Taft didn't answer but went straight to a vacant chair at the dining room table and sat down. She was clearly upset and at a loss for words. Mrs. Dunnigan silently put cups of fresh coffee in front of her and John Shaw and Uncle Ned. No one seemed to want to talk.

Celia finally got the nerve to speak. "Mrs. Taft, how is Mandie? Please tell me the truth." Her eyes clouded with tears.

Mrs. Taft took a deep breath, drank a big swallow of the coffee, and finally replied with tears in her eyes. "Oh, Celia, she is still unconscious, and they can't seem to get her back. I went over all the tests they have done and the only thing they found was a broken wrist—her left one."

"Oh no," Celia moaned.

"The doctors have set it, but I imagine it will be a while before she can use it to write. But that is the least of our concerns," Mrs. Taft explained.

"Have you been to the college, Mrs. Taft?" Grace asked.

Mrs. Taft looked at her, evidently wondering who she was.

"I'm sorry. I'm Grace Wilson and I am in some classes with Mandie," Grace explained.

Mrs. Taft's face softened into recognition. "Oh, you are Grace Wilson. I have heard your name before. And to answer your question, no, I have not been to the college, but rest assured as soon as I can get my energy back I'll be taking that place apart."

The three girls looked at each other and discreetly smiled.

"Please tell me exactly what happened, Celia. You were with Mandie at the time of the accident, were you not?"

"Yes, ma'am, I was," Celia replied.

But before she could continue, Mary Lou quickly interrupted. "And thanks to Celia, the horse and carriage was brought under control."

Mrs. Taft gave Celia a pleased smile, causing Celia to blush. "I only grabbed the reins when Mr. Ryland fell out," she said, then continued, "Mrs. Taft, those girls who neglected to help after the accident are the same girls who have been so rude with Mandie and me. I don't know who the girl was driving the motorcar—I had never seen her or the motorcar before. She had her motorcar taking up several parking spaces, and when Mandie told her to move, she rammed the motorcar into our carriage—and then the horse went wild. Mr. Ryland fell out when the carriage hit a rock wall and Mandie got knocked out in the carriage somehow when the horse went running wild."

"Then you managed to get the horse to stop," Mrs. Taft concluded. "Did any of those girls at the college offer to help?"

"No, ma'am," she said, glancing at Mary Lou, who nodded for her to tell the whole story. "They started laughing and making fun of Mandie and you, saying Mandie caused it all by being so snooty and rich, as they called it."

"Mrs. Taft," Mary Lou spoke up, "Grace and I were standing there waiting for Mandie to pick me up and we saw and heard everything. Those girls acted like heathens."

"I wonder why they are so hostile toward Mandie," Mrs. Taft said.

"They said terrible things about you, too," Mary Lou reminded her. "Like you are so high and mighty and all that kind of stuff."

"Oh dear, where did they get that idea?" Mrs. Taft wondered aloud.

John Shaw finally spoke. "Sounds like jealousy to me."

Mrs. Taft looked at him. "Jealousy?"

"Yes, you see, since you are Mandie's grandmother and you are so wealthy, she can have anything she wants," he explained.

"But I don't give her everything she wants," Mrs. Taft protested. "Only what I think she should have."

John Shaw grinned and said, "Which is *more* than she ever wants."

"Now, John, I want her to be happy and comfortable in life," Mrs. Taft insisted.

Uncle Ned had not said a word, but now he spoke. "Papoose give lots to Cherokee people. People love her. Why white people so mean?" He looked very sad.

"Jealousy," John Shaw repeated. "They can't stand for her to have more than they do."

There was a rapid knock on the front door, and everyone came to attention. Mr. Dunnigan hurried to open it, and since the front door was visible from the dining room, they could see it was an employee from the hospital.

"Good day, sir. Dr. Zeager sent me to tell you that Miss Amanda Shaw is awake and talking now."

Shouts of joy and thanks came from everyone in the dining room.

"Come in," Mr. Dunnigan told the man.

"I'm sorry, sir, but I have to return to the hospital for other duties," the man said. "Dr. Zeager wanted you to know that you may bring Miss Shaw home any time you get ready. Good day, sir." The man quickly left.

Mr. Dunnigan closed the front door and came back to the dining room to find John Shaw and Uncle Ned already standing. "If you would please take us over there, Mr. Donovan, we will bring her here," Mr. Shaw requested.

"Yes, sir," Mr. Donovan agreed.

By the time Mrs. Dunnigan put pillows and a coverlet on the sofa in the parlor, they were back. Mandie was insisting she could walk, but John Shaw insisted he carry her into the house and deposit her on the settee.

Everyone was talking at once. Mandie had tears in her eyes and reached for her grandmother's hand. "You came," she said in a shaky voice.

"Of course I came. After all, you were my only granddaughter for fifteen years. You are still my special one, dear, and will always be."

"And you are special, too, Grandmother," Mandie answered. Glancing around the room she said, "Now, can somebody please tell me what happened? I wake up suddenly and find myself in a hospital with no one around that I even know!"

"Do you not remember any of it?" Celia asked.

Mandie shook her head, but as Mary Lou, Celia, and Grace repeated the events, Mandie began to remember them. "You stopped the horse from running away! Oh," Mandie said to Celia, "you are over your fright of horses."

Celia grinned and said, "But I'd rather for it to have happened some other way."

"Will poor Mr. Ryland be all right?" Mandie asked.

"Oh yes, I checked on him," Grace answered. "The doctor said he was very lucky. I suppose he'll be wanting you to get another carriage so he can go back to work, even with a broken arm."

Mandie glanced at her grandmother. "Mr. Ryland is a wonderful man, Grandmother," she said. "Do you think we could get another carriage for him to use during the summer while we are home on vacation?"

"Of course, dear, I'll see about it tomorrow," Mrs. Taft said. "I'll also check and see if his family needs anything in the meantime while he isn't working." She straightened up in her chair and suddenly changed her tone of voice. "I will also be checking to see what can be done about those uncivilized girls at the college."

Mandie looked directly at Uncle Ned and said, "I thought we were supposed to do good for evil."

Uncle Ned smiled, nodded his head, and said, "Papoose learning to think first."

Mrs. Taft said firmly, "Amanda, we cannot let something like this happen and not do anything about it. If we let it go there may be more incidents, maybe more serious. I just want to discuss this matter with the college president."

"Yes, ma'am," Mandie meekly agreed. "But I believe the girls will get even worse if we report them."

"Well, if they do, I can guarantee they will be expelled," Mrs. Taft said. She looked across the room at Mr. Donovan and asked, "Would it be possible for you to drive us to the carriage factory, Mr. Ryland's home, and the college tomorrow?"

"Of course, I am at your service, Mrs. Taft," Mr. Donovan assured her. "Where shall I pick you up and when?"

Mrs. Dunnigan immediately said, "Mrs. Taft, we insist you and Mr. Shaw and Uncle Ned stay here with us while you are in town. We have plenty of bedrooms."

"Thank you, Mrs. Dunnigan, I accept your offer with many thanks," Mrs. Taft replied.

"So do I," John Shaw said. Looking at Uncle Ned he asked, "You too?"

Uncle Ned nodded and said, "Must stay a day or two to see if Papoose get in more trouble." He smiled at Mandie.

Mrs. Dunnigan had the girls help her get the rooms ready while Mr. Donovan went to the depot to get Mrs. Taft's luggage, then to the law enforcement's stables, where John Shaw and Uncle Ned had left their baggage with their horses.

The next morning Mrs. Taft's first stop was at the college. Mandie dreaded facing those girls who were so rude after the accident. Luckily, Mrs. Taft had timed their visit to see the president while everyone was in chapel.

"Come along, Amanda," Mrs. Taft said as she went straight to the door marked *President*. She tapped on the frosted glass pane, then opened the door. The name on the door was Miss Clara Trellain.

Mandie had never seen the president of the school, and when she looked into the room, she saw a younger woman with golden light-brown hair. The woman smiled as she stood up when the ladies came into the room.

"Welcome, Mrs. Taft," the woman greeted her as she offered her hand. Then she looked at Mandie and said, "I'm so sorry I have not had the pleasure of meeting you, Miss Shaw. Since you have not been living in the dormitory, we don't see much of you."

Mandie nodded her head.

"Please sit down," the woman said, indicating chairs and a small settee in the room.

As soon as they were seated, Mrs. Taft started right into her complaint concerning the girls who had neglected to help after the accident. Mandie was irritated to notice that the woman smiled during the whole story. So she evidently thought it was nothing to worry about.

When Mrs. Taft finished, she said, "I want something done about these girls immediately. I will not stand for this."

"Yes, I know, Mrs. Taft, but something has already been done about it," Miss Trellain said. "You see, all the girls came in to see me yesterday afternoon and we had quite a conversation regarding this. They were all so very apologetic and wanted to know what they should do. I told them nothing short of a sincere apology to Miss Shaw would be acceptable. They are waiting to see her, but since we didn't know when she would come home from the hospital, the girls have been waiting in the dormitory. So if you both would come with me, we will go up there and give them an opportunity to express their regrets."

Mrs. Taft rose and followed her as she said, "They had better have sincere regrets."

Mandie hated facing the girls with her grandmother. She had no idea what Mrs. Taft might say or do and worried it might make matters worse, but she followed the two ladies anyway.

When they walked into the sitting room of the dormitory, a crowd of girls greeted them with "Hello, Mandie" and "We're glad you're back." Then one by one the girls said that they were sorry for what happened and for saying such mean things. They admitted to her that they were jealous and threatened by her because of the amazing opportunities she has had in her life so far.

Mandie didn't know exactly what to do, so she just said, "Your apologies are accepted," and turned and hastily left the room. She ran down the huge marble staircase and was surprised when the girls followed her.

When she got to the bottom of the stairs she stopped and said, "All right, you are forgiven. Just please stop following me."

Mandie turned and ran up to the road where Mr. Donovan was waiting with his carriage. She jumped into the seat and waited for her grandmother to catch up with her.

Suddenly George Stuart appeared and saw Mandie sitting alone in the carriage. He walked up to her and said, "Sorry I cannot speak to you; we haven't been properly introduced yet."

His sister, who had been walking with him, stepped forward and said, "Amanda Shaw, I would like for you to meet my brother, George Stuart."

George bowed and said, "I am very honored to make the acquaintance of Miss Amanda Shaw, the heroine of the hour. Miss Shaw, may I have the honor of being your escort for the final social this year?" He straightened up and waited.

Mandie realized he was really asking her to be his escort at the school banquet. She smiled at him and said, "I shall give it some consideration and give you my answer within a fortnight."

"Thank you, Miss Shaw," George Stuart said.

At that moment Mrs. Taft arrived at the carriage and told Mr. Donovan, "We should go on to the carriage factory now, if you please."

Mr. Donovan helped her into the carriage as Mandie tried to

keep the shocked yet excited look off her face.

"Miss Trellain will arrange for you to take your final examinations orally since you cannot use your hand to write," Mrs. Taft told her. "And those girls sounded quite sincere in their apologies; I hope they're people you can be friendly with now."

Mandie was just overwhelmed and needed some time away from the college.

———

When Mandie and Mrs. Taft had finished their errands for the day, they returned to the Dunnigans', where good news was awaiting Mandie. Her mother had called the law enforcement office and left word that Mandie should not make any arrangements for the end of the school year about visiting her friends. Elizabeth Shaw said that she and John Shaw would be checking Mandie out of school when the year ended, and then they were going to stay at the beach cottage belonging to their friends the Pattons, who would be out of town. Mandie and her mother and her uncle would have two whole weeks together alone, without the babies, and without all those friends Mandie was forever congregating with.

When Mrs. Dunnigan gave Mandie the message, Mandie was more excited than she had ever been about anything. She was going to have her mother and Uncle John all to herself. Everyone seemed to be congregating all the time at some place or other, and she was rather tired of it. She had never had her mother and Uncle John all to herself for any length of time before.

She could hardly wait for the school year to end.

And then she remembered something—Adrian. What would she do if Adrian arrived and tried to catch up with her? She still wasn't sure whether she wanted to see him or not. She'd think about it and decide by the time school was out for the summer, which was only two weeks away.

And then there was Joe. Was he planning to come down to travel home with her when school let out?

And she couldn't believe that she had finally been asked out by George Stuart. What would become of him over the summer?

Oh, so many things that needed answers. But for now Mandie was going to enjoy the last two weeks of school with her friends.